LADDERS TO FIRE

Ladders to Fire

By Anaïs Nin

THE SWALLOW PRESS INC.
CHICAGO

Published by
The Swallow Press Incorporated
811 West Junior Terrace
Chicago, Illinois 60613

ISBN (PAPERBOUND EDITION) 0-8040-0181-2
LIBRARY OF CONGRESS CATALOG CARD NUMBER 66-6834

THIS HUNGER

LILLIAN was always in a state of fermentation. Her eyes rent the air and left phosphorescent streaks. Her large teeth were lustful. One thought of a negress who had found a secret potion to turn her skin white and her hair red.

As soon as she came into a room she kicked off her shoes. Necklaces and buttons choked her and she loosened them, scarves strangled her and she slackened them. Her hand bag was always bursting full and often spilled over.

She was always in full movement, in the center of a whirlpool of people, letters, and telephones. She was always poised on the pinnacle of a drama, a problem, a conflict. She seemed to trapeze from one climax to another, from one paroxysm of anxiety to another, skipping always the peaceful region in between, the deserts and the pauses. One marvelled that she slept, for this was a suspension of activity. One felt sure that in her sleep she twitched and rolled, and even fell off the bed, or that she slept half sitting up as if caught while still talking. And one felt certain that a great combat had taken place during the night, displacing the covers and pillows.

When she cooked, the entire kitchen was galvanized by the strength she put into it; the dishes, pans, knives, everything bore the brunt of her strength, everything was violently marshalled, challenged, forced to bloom, to cook, to boil. The vegetables were peeled as if the skins were torn from their resisting flesh, as if they were the fur of animals being peeled by the hunters. The fruit was stabbed, assassinated, the lettuce was murdered with a machete. The flavoring was poured like hot lava and one expected the salad to wither, shrivel instantly. The bread was sliced with a vigor which recalled heads falling from the guillotine. The bottles and glasses were knocked hard against each other as in bowling games, so that the wine, beer and water were conquered before they reached the table.

What was concocted in this cuisine reminded one of the sword swallowers at the fair, the fire-eaters and the glass-eaters of the Hindu magic sects. The same chemicals were used in the cooking as were used in the composition of her own being: only those which caused the most violent reaction, contradiction, and teasing, the refusal to answer questions but the love of putting them, and all the strong spices of human relationship which bore a relation to black pepper, paprika, soybean sauce, ketchup and red peppers. In a laboratory she would have caused explosions. In life she caused them and was afterwards aghast at the damage. Then she would hurriedly set about to atone for the havoc, for the miscarried phrase, the fatal honesty, the reckless act, the disrupting scene, the explosive and catastrophic attack. Everywhere, after the storms of her appearance, there was emotional devastation. Contacts were broken, faiths withered, fatal revelations made. Harmony, illusion, equilibrium were annihilated. The next day she herself was amazed to see friendships all askew, like pictures after an earthquake.

The storms of doubt, the quick cloudings of hypersensitivity, the bursts of laughter, the wet furred voice charged with electrical vibrations, the resonant quality of her movements, left many echoes and vibrations in the air. The curtains continued to move after she left. The furniture was warm, the air was whirling, the mirrors were scarred from the exigent way she extracted from them an ever satisfactory image of herself.

Her red hair was as unruly as her whole self; no comb could dress it. No dress would cling and mould her, but every inch of it would stand out like ruffled feathers. Tumult in orange, red and yellow and green quarreling with each other. The rose devoured the orange, the green and blue overwhelmed the purple. The sport jacket was irritated to be in company with the silk dress, the tailored coat at war with the embroidery, the every-day shoes at variance with the turquoise bracelet. And if at times she chose a majestic hat, it sailed precariously like a sailboat on a choppy sea.

Did she dream of being the appropriate mate for the Centaur, for the Viking, for the Pioneer, for Attila or Genghis Khan, of being magnificently mated with Conquerors, the Inquisitioners or Emperors?

On the contrary. In the center of this turmoil, she gave birth to the dream of a ghost lover, a pale, passive, romantic, anaemic figure garbed in grey and timidity. Out of the very volcano of her strength she gave birth to the most evanescent, delicate and unreachable image.

She saw him first of all in a dream, and the second time while under the effects of ether. His pale face appeared, smiled, vanished. He haunted her sleep and her unconscious self.

The third time he appeared in person in the street. Friends

introduced them. She felt the shock of familiarity known to lovers.

He stood exactly as in the dream, smiling, passive, static. He had a way of greeting that seemed more like a farewell, an air of being on his way.

She fell in love with an extinct volcano.

Her strength and fire were aroused. Her strength flowed around his stillness, encircled his silence, encompassed his quietness.

She invited him. He consented. Her whirlpool nature eddied around him, agitating the fixed, saturnian orbit.

"Do you want to come . . . do you?"

"I never know what I want," he smiled because of her emphasis on the "want," "I do not go out very much." From the first, into this void created by his not wanting, she was to throw her own desires, but not meet an answer, merely a pliability which was to leave her in doubt forever as to whether she had substituted her desire for his. From the first she was to play the lover alone, giving the questions and the answers too.

When man imposes his will on woman, she knows how to give him the pleasure of assuming his power is greater and his will becomes her pleasure; but when the woman accomplishes this, the man never gives her a feeling of any pleasure, only of guilt for having spoken first and reversed the roles. Very often she was to ask: "Do you want to do this?" And he did not know. She would fill the void, for the sake of filling it, for the sake of advancing, moving, feeling, and then he implied: "You are pushing me."

When he came to see her he was enigmatic. But he was there.

As she felt the obstacle, she also felt the force of her love, its impetus striking the obstacle, the impact of the resistance. This collision seemed to her the reality of passion.

He had been there a few moments and was already preparing for flight, looking at the geography of the room, marking the exits "in case of fire," when the telephone rang.

"It's Serge asking me to go to a concert," said Lillian with the proper feminine inflection of: "I shall do your will, not mine." And this time Gerard, although he was not openly and violently in favor of Lillian, was openly against Serge, whoever he was. He showed hostility. And Lillian interpreted this favorably. She refused the invitation and felt as if Gerard had declared his passion. She laid down the telephone as if marking a drama and sat nearer to the Gerard who had manifested his jealousy.

The moment she sat near him he recaptured his quality of a mirage: paleness, otherworldliness, obliqueness. He appropriated woman's armor and defences, and she took the man's. Lillian was the lover seduced by obstacle and the dream. Gerard watched her fire with a feminine delectation of all fires caused by seduction.

When they kissed she was struck with ecstasy and he with fear.

Gerard was fascinated and afraid. He was in danger of being possessed. Why in danger? Because he was already possessed by his mother and two possessions meant annihilation.

Lillian could not understand. They were two different loves, and could not interfere with each other.

She saw, however, that Gerard was paralyzed, that the very thought of the two loves confronting each other meant death.

He retreated. The next day he was ill, ill with terror. He sought to explain. "I have to take care of my mother."

"Well," said Lillian, "I will help you."

This did not reassure him. At night he had nightmares. There was a resemblance between the two natures, and to possess Lillian was like possessing the mother, which was taboo. Besides, in the nightmare, there was a battle between the two possessions in which he won nothing but a change of masters. Because both his mother and Lillian (in the nightmare they were confused and indistinguishable), instead of living out their own thoughts, occupying their own hands, playing their own instruments, put all their strength, wishes, desires, their wills on him. He felt that in the nightmare they carved him out like a statue, they talked for him, they acted for him, they fought for him, they never let him alone. He was merely the possessed. He was not free.

Lillian, like his mother, was too strong for him. The battle between the two women would be too strong for him. He could not separate them, free himself and make his choice. He was at a disadvantage. So he feared: he feared his mother and the outcries, the scenes, dramas, and he feared Lillian for the same reason since they were of the same elements: fire and water and aggression. So he feared the new invasion which endangered the pale little flame of his life. In the center of his being there was no strength to answer the double challenge. The only alternative was retreat.

When he was six years old he had asked his mother for the secret of how children were born. His mother answered: "I made you."

"You made me?" Gerard repeated in utter wonder. Then he had stood before a mirror and marvelled: "You made this hair? You made this skin?"

"Yes," said his mother. "I made them."

"How difficult it must have been, and my nose! And my teeth! And you made me walk, too." He was lost in admiration of his mother. He believed her. But after a moment of gazing at the mirror he said: "There is one thing I can't believe. I can't believe that you made my eyes!"

His eyes. Even today when his mother was still making him, directing him, when she cut his hair, fashioned him, carved him, watched his clothes, what was left free in this encirclement of his being were his eyes. He could not act, but he could see.

But his retreat was inarticulate, negative, baffling to Lillian. When she was hurt, baffled, lost, she in turn retreated, then he renewed his pursuit of her. For he loved her strength and would have liked it for himself. When this strength did not threaten him, when the danger was removed, then he gave way to his attraction for this strength. Then he pursued it. He invited and lured it back, he would not surrender it (to Serge or anyone else). And Lillian who suffered from his retreat suffered even more from his mysterious returns, and his pursuits which ceased as soon as she responded to them.

He was playing with his fascination and his fear.

When she turned her back on him, he renewed his charms, enchanted her and won her back. Feminine wiles used against woman's strength like women's ambivalent evasions and returns. Wiles of which Lillian, with her straightforward manly soul, knew nothing.

The obstacle only aroused Lillian's strength (as it aroused the knights of old) but the obstacle discouraged Gerard and killed his desire. The obstacle became his alibi for weakness. The obstacle for Gerard was insurmountable. As soon as Lillian overcame one, Gerard erected another. By all these diversions and perversions of the truth he preserved from her and from himself the secret of his weakness. The secret was kept. The web of delusion grew around their love. To preserve this fatal secret: you, Lillian, are too strong; you, Gerard, are not strong enough (which would destroy them), Gerard (like a woman) wove false pretexts. The false pretexts did not deceive Lillian. She knew there was a deeper truth but she did not know what it was.

Weary of fighting the false pretexts she turned upon herself and her own weakness, her self-doubts, suddenly betrayed her. Gerard had awakened the dormant demon doubt. To defend his weakness he had unknowingly struck at her. So Lillian began to think: "I did not arouse his love. I was not beautiful enough." And she began to make a long list of self-accusations. Then the harm was done. She had been the aggressor so she was the more seriously wounded. Self-doubt asserted itself. The seed of doubt was implanted in Lillian to work its havoc with time. The real Gerard receded, faded, vanished, and was reinstated as a dream image. Other Gerards will appear, until . . .

⁘

After the disappearance of Gerard, Lillian resumed her defensive attitude towards man, and became again the warrior. It became absolutely essential to her to triumph in the smallest issue of an argument. Because she felt so insecure about her own value it became of vital importance to convince and win over everyone to her assertions. So she could not bear to yield, to be convinced, defeated, persuaded, swerved in the little things.

She was now afraid to yield to passion, and because she could not yield to the larger impulses it became essential also to not yield to the small ones, even if her adversary were in the right. She was living on a plane of war. The bigger resistance to the flow of life became one with the smaller resistance to the will of others, and the smallest issue became equal to the ultimate one. The pleasure of yielding on a level of passion being unknown to her, the pleasure of yielding on other levels became equally impossible. She denied herself all the sources of feminine pleasure: of being invaded, of being conquered. In war, conquest was imperative. No approach from the enemy could be interpreted as anything but a threat. She could not see that the real issue of the war was a defense of her being against the invasion of passion. Her enemy was the lover who might possess her. All her intensity was poured into the small battles; to win in the choice of a restaurant, of a movie, of visitors, in opinions, in analysis of people, to win in all the small rivalries through an evening.

At the same time as this urge to triumph continuously, she felt no appeasement or pleasure from her victories. What she won was not what she really wanted. Deep down, what her nature wanted was to be made to yield.

The more she won (and she won often for no man withstood this guerrilla warfare with any honors — he could not see the great importance that a picture hung to the left rather than to the right might have) the more unhappy and empty she felt.

No great catastrophe threatened her. She was not tragically struck down as others were by the death of a loved one at war. There was no visible enemy, no real tragedy, no hospital, no cemetery, no mortuary, no morgue, no criminal court, no crime, no horror. There was nothing.

She was traversing a street. The automobile did not strike her down. It was not she who was inside of the ambulance being delivered to St. Vincent's Hospital. It was not she whose mother died. It was not she whose brother was killed in the war.

In all the registers of catastrophe her name did not appear. She was not attacked, raped, or mutilated. She was not kidnapped for white slavery.

But as she crossed the street and the wind lifted the dust, just before it touched her face, she felt as if all these horrors had happened to her, she felt the nameless anguish, the shrinking of the heart, the asphyxiation of pain, the horror of torture whose cries no one hears.

Every other sorrow, illness, or pain is understood, pitied, shared with all human beings. Not this one which was mysterious and solitary.

It was ineffectual, inarticulate, unmoving to others as the attempted crying out of the mute.

Everybody understands hunger, illness, poverty, slavery and torture. No one understood that at this moment at which she crossed the street with every privilege granted her, of not being hungry, of not being imprisoned or tortured, all these privileges were a subtler form of torture. They were given to her, the house, the complete family, the food, the loves, like a mirage. Given and denied. They were present to the eyes of others who said: "You are fortunate," and invisible to her. Because the anguish, the mysterious poison, corroded all of them, distorted the relationships, blighted the food, haunted the house, installed war where there was no apparent war, torture where there was no sign of instruments, and enemies where there were no enemies to capture and defeat.

Anguish was a voiceless woman screaming in a nightmare.

⁘

She stood waiting for Lillian at the door. And what struck Lillian instantly was the aliveness of Djuna: if only Gerard had been like her! Their meeting was like a joyous encounter of equal forces.

Djuna responded instantly to the quick rhythm, to the intensity. It was a meeting of equal speed, equal fervor, equal strength. It was as if they had been two champion skiers making simultaneous jumps and landing together at the same spot. It was like a meeting of two chemicals exactly balanced, fusing and foaming with the pleasure of achieved proportions.

Lillian knew that Djuna would not sit peacefully or passively in her room awaiting the knock on her door, perhaps not hearing it the first time, or hearing it and walking casually towards it. She knew Djuna would have her door open and would be there when the elevator deposited her. And Djuna knew by the swift approach of Lillian that Lillian would have the answer to her alert curiosity, to her impatience; that she would hasten the elevator trip, quicken the journey, slide over the heavy carpet in time to meet this wave of impatience and enthusiasm.

Just as there are elements which are sensitive to change and climate and rise fast to higher temperatures, there were in Lillian and Djuna rhythms which left them both suspended in utter solitude. It was not in body alone that they arrived on time for their meetings, but they arrived primed for high living, primed for flight, for explosion, for ecstasy, for feeling, for all experience.

The slowness of others in starting, their slowness in answering, caused them often to soar alone.

To Djuna Lillian answered almost before she spoke, answered with her bristling hair and fluttering hands, and the tinkle of her jewelry.

"Gerard lost everything when he lost you," said Djuna before Lillian had taken off her coat. "He lost life."

Lillian was trying to recapture an impression she had before seeing Djuna. "Why, Djuna, when I heard your voice over the telephone I thought you were delicate and fragile. And you look fragile but somehow not weak. I came to . . . well, to protect you. I don't know what from."

Djuna laughed. She had enormous fairytale eyes, like two aquamarine lights illumining darkness, eyes of such depth that at first one felt one might fall into them as into a sea, a sea of feeling. And then they ceased to be the pulling, drawing, absorbing sea and they became beacons, with extraordinary intensity of vision, of awareness, of perception. Then one felt one's chaos illumined, transfigured. Where the blue, liquid balls alighted every object acquired significance.

At the same time their vulnerability and sentience made them tremble like the delicate candlelight or like the eye of the finest camera lens which at too intense daylight will suddenly shut black. One caught the inner chamber like the photographer's dark room, in which sensitivity to daylight, to crudity and grossness would cause instantaneous annihilation of the image.

They gave the impression of a larger vision of the world. If sensitivity made them retract, contract swiftly, it was not in any self-protective blindness but to turn again to that inner chamber where the metamorphosis took place and in which the pain became not personal, but the pain of the whole world, in which ugliness became not a personal experience of ugliness but the world's experience with all ugliness. By enlarging and situating it in the totality of the dream, the unbearable event became a large, airy understanding of life which gave to her eyes an ultimately triumphant power which people mistook for strength, but which was in reality courage. For the eyes, wounded on the exterior, turned inward, but did not stay there, and returned with the renewed vision. After each encounter with naked unbearable truths, naked unbearable pain, the eyes returned to the mirrors in the inner chambers, to the transformation by understanding and reflection, so that they could emerge and face the naked truth again.

In the inner chambers there was a treasure room. In it dwelt her racial wealth of Byzantine imagery, a treasure room of hierarchic figures, religious symbols. Old men of religion, who had assisted at her birth and blessed her with their wisdom. They appeared in the colors of death, because they had at first endangered her advance into life. Their robes, their caps, were made of the heavily embroidered materials of rituals illumined with the light of eternity. They had willed her their wisdom of life and death, of past and future, and therefore excluded the present. Wisdom was a swifter way of reaching death. Death was postponed by living, by suffering, by risking, by losing, by error. These men of religion had at first endangered her life, for their wisdom had incited her in the past to forgo the human test of experience, to forgo the error and the confusion which was living. By knowing she would reach all, not by touching, not by way of the body. There had lurked in these secret chambers of her ancestry a subtle threat such as lurked in all the temples, synagogues, churches – the incense of denial, the perfume of the body burnt to sacrificial ashes by religious alchemy, transmuted into guilt and atonement.

In the inner chamber there were also other figures. The mother madonna holding the child and nourishing it. The haunting mother image forever holding a small child.

Then there was the child itself, the child inhabiting a world of peaceful, laughing animals, rich trees, in valleys of festive color. The child in her eyes appeared with its eyes closed. It was dreaming the fertile valleys, the small warm house, the Byzantine flowers, the tender animals and the abundance. It was dreaming and afraid to awaken. It was dreaming the lightness of the sky, the warmth of the earth, the fecundity of the colors.

It was afraid to awaken.

∴

Lillian's vivid presence filled the hotel room. She was so entirely palpable, visible, present. She was not parcelled into a woman who was partly in the past and partly in the future, or one whose spirit was partly at home with her children, and partly elsewhere. She was here, all of her, eyes and ears, and hands and warmth and interest and alertness, with a sympathy which surrounded Djuna – questioned, investigated, absorbed, saw, heard. . . .

"You give me something wonderful, Lillian. A feeling that I have a friend. Let's have dinner here. Let's celebrate."

Voices charged with emotion. Fullness. To be able to talk as one feels. To be able to say all.

"I lost Gerard because I leaped. I expressed my feelings. He was afraid. Why do I love men who are afraid? He was afraid and I had to court him. Djuna, did you ever think how men who court a woman and do not win her are not hurt? And woman gets hurt. If woman plays the Don Juan and does the courting and the man retreats she is mutilated in some way."

"Yes, I have noticed that. I suppose it's a kind of guilt. For a man it is natural to be the aggressor and he takes defeat well. For woman it is a transgression, and she assumes the defeat is caused by the aggression. How long will woman be ashamed of her strength?"

"Djuna, take this."

She handed her a silver medallion she was wearing.

"Well, you didn't win Gerard but you shook him out of his death."

"Why," said Lillian, "aren't men as you are?"

"I was thinking the same thing," said Djuna.

"Perhaps when they are we don't like them or fear them. Perhaps we like the ones who are not strong. . . ."

Lillian found this relation to Djuna palpable and joyous. There was in them a way of asserting its reality, by constant signs, gifts, expressiveness, words, letters, telephones, an exchange of visible affection, palpable responses. They exchanged jewels, clothes, books, they protected each other, they expressed concern, jealousy, possessiveness. They talked. The relationship was the central, essential personage of this dream without pain. This relationship had the aspect of a primitive figure to which both enjoyed presenting proofs of worship and devotion. It was an active, continuous ceremony in which there entered no moments of indifference, fatigue, or misunderstandings or separations, no eclipses, no doubts.

"I wish you were a man," Lillian often said.

"I wish you were."

Outwardly it was Lillian who seemed more capable of this metamorphosis. She had the physical strength, the physical dynamism, the physical appearance of strength. She carried tailored clothes well; her gestures were direct and violent. Masculinity seemed more possible to her, outwardly. Yet inwardly she was in a state of chaos and confusion. Inwardly she was like nature, chaotic and irrational. She had no vision into this chaos: it ruled her and swamped her. It sucked her into miasmas, into hurricanes, into caverns of blind suffering.

Outwardly Djuna was the essence of femininity . . . a curled frilled flower which might have been a starched undulating petticoat or a ruffled ballet skirt moulded into a sea shell. But inwardly the nature was clarified, ordered, understood, dominated. As a child Djuna had looked upon the storms of her own nature — jealousy, anger, resentment — always with the knowledge that they could be dominated, that she refused to be devastated by them, or to destroy others with them. As a child, alone, of her own free will, she had taken on an oriental attitude of dominating her nature by wisdom and understanding. Finally, with the use of every known instrument — art, aesthetic forms, philosophy, psychology — it had been tamed.

But each time she saw it in Lillian, flaring, uncontrolled, wild, blind, destroying itself and others, her compassion and love were aroused. "That will be my gift to her," she thought with warmth, with pity. "I will guide her."

Meanwhile Lillian was exploring this aesthetic, this form, this mystery that was Djuna. She was taking up Djuna's clothes one by one, amazed at their complication, their sheer femininity. "Do you wear this?" she asked, looking at the black lace nightgown. "I thought only prostitutes wore this!"

She investigated the perfumes, the cosmetics, the refined coquetries, the veils, the muffs, the scarves. She was almost like a sincere and simple person before a world of artifice. She was afraid of being deceived by all this artfulness. She could not see it as aesthetic, but as the puritans see it: as deception, as immorality, as belonging with seduction and eroticism.

She insisted on seeing Djuna without make-up, and was then satisfied that make-up was purely an enhancement of the features, not treachery.

⁂

Lillian's house was beautiful, lacquered, grown among the trees, and bore the mark of her handiwork all through, yet it did not seem to belong to her. She had painted, decorated, carved, arranged, selected, and most of it was made by her own hands, or refashioned, always touched or handled or improved by her, out of her very own activity and craftsmanship. Yet it did not become her house, and it did not have her face, her atmosphere. She always looked like a stranger in it. With all her handiwork and taste, she had not been able to give it her own character.

It was a home; it suited her husband, Larry, and her children. It was built for peace. The rooms were spacious, clear, brightly windowed. It was warm, glowing, clean, harmonious. It was like other houses.

As soon as Djuna entered it, she felt this. The strength, the fervor, the care Lillian spent in the house, on her husband and children came from some part of her being that was not the deepest Lillian. It was as if every element but her own nature had contributed to create this life. Who had made the marriage? Who had desired the children? She could not remember the first impetus, the first choice, the first desire for these, nor how they came to be. It was as if it had happened in her sleep. Lillian, guided by her background, her mother, her sisters, her habits, her home as a child, her blindness in regard to her own desires, had made all this and then lived in it, but it had not been made out of the deeper elements of her nature, and she was a stranger in it.

Once made—this life, these occupations, the care, the devotion, the family—it never occurred to her that she could rebel against them. There was no provocation for rebellion. Her husband was kind, her children were lovable, her house was harmonious; and Nanny, the old nurse who took care of them all with inexhaustible maternal warmth, was their guardian angel, the guardian angel of the home.

Nanny's devotion to the home was so strong, so predominant, and so constantly manifested that the home and family seemed to belong to her more than to Lillian. The home had a reality for Nanny. Her whole existence was centered on it. She defended its interests, she hovered, reigned, watched, guarded tirelessly. She passed judgments on the visitors. Those who were dangerous to the peace of the home, she served with unappetizing meals, and from one end of the meal to the other, showed her disapproval. The welcome ones were those her instinct told her were good for the family, the home, for their unity. Then she surpassed herself in cooking and service. The unity of the family was her passionate concern: that the children should understand each other and love each other; that the children should love the father, the mother; that the mother and father should be close. For this she was willing to be the receiver of confidences, to be the peace maker, to reestablish order.

She was willing to show an interest in any of Lillian's activities as long as these ultimately flowed back to the house. She could be interested in concerts if she brought the overflow of the music home to enhance it. She could be interested in painting while the results showed visibly in the house.

When the conversation lagged at the table she supplied diversion. If the children quarrelled she upheld the rights of each one in soothing, wise explanations.

She refused one proposal of marriage.

When Lillian came into the house, and felt lost in it, unable to really enter into, to feel it, to participate, to care, as if it were all not present and warm but actually a family album, as if her son Paul did not come in and really take off his snow-covered boots, but it was a snapshot of Paul taking off his boots, as if her husband's face were a photograph too, and Adele was actually the painting of her above the piano . . . then Lillian rushed to the kitchen, unconsciously seeking Nanny's worries, Nanny's anxieties (Paul is too thin, and Adele lost her best friend in school) to convince herself of the poignant reality of this house and its occupants (her husband had forgotten his rubbers).

If the children had not been growing up (again according to Nanny's tabulations and calculations) Lillian would have thought herself back ten years. Her husband did not change.

Nanny was the only one who had felt the shock the day that Lillian decided to have her own room. And Lillian might not have changed the rooms over if it had not been for a cricket.

Lilian's husband had gone away on a trip. It was summer. Lillian felt deeply alone, and filled with anxiety. She could not understand the anxiety. Her first thought always was: Larry is happy. He is well. He looked very happy when he left. The children are well. Then what can be the matter with me? How can anything be the matter with me if they are well?

There were guests at the house. Among them was one who vaguely resembled Gerard, and the young man in her dreams, and the young man who appeared to her under anaesthetic. Always of the same family. But he was bold as a lover. He courted her swiftly, impetuously.

A cricket had lodged itself in one of the beams of her room. Perfectly silent until the young man came to visit her, until he caressed her. Then it burst into frenzied cricket song.

They laughed.

He came again the next night, and at the same moment the cricket sang again.

Always at the moment a cricket should sing.

The young man went away. Larry returned. Larry was happy to be with his wife.

But the cricket did not sing. Lillian wept. Lillian moved into a room of her own. Nanny was depressed and cross for a week.

⁘

When they sat together, alone, in the evenings, Larry did not appear to see her. When he talked about her he always talked about the Lillian of ten years ago; how she looked then, how she was, what she said. He delighted in reviving scenes out of the past, her behaviour, her high temper and the troubles she got herself into. He often repeated these stories. And Lillian felt that she had known only one Larry, a Larry who had courted her and then remained as she had first known him. When she heard about the Lillian of ten years ago she felt no connection with her. But Larry was living with her, delighting in her presence. He reconstructed her out of his memory and sat her there every evening they had together.

One night they heard a commotion in the otherwise peaceful village. The police car passed and then the ambulance. Then the family doctor stopped his car before the gate. He asked for a drink. "My job is over," he said, "and I need a drink badly." Lillian gave him one, but at first he would not talk.

Later he explained: The man who rented the house next door was a young doctor, not a practicing one. His behaviour and way of living had perplexed the neighbors. He received no one, allowed no one into the house. He was somber in mood, and attitude, and he was left alone. But people complained persistently of an unbearable odor. There were investigations. Finally it was discovered that his wife had died six months earlier, in California. He had brought her body back and he was living with it stretched on his bed. The doctor had seen her.

Lillian left the room. The odor of death, the image of death . . . everywhere.

No investigation would be made in her house. No change. Nanny was there.

But Lillian felt trapped without knowing what had trapped her.

Then she found Djuna. With Djuna she was alive. With Djuna her entire being burst into living, flowering cells. She could feel her own existence, the Lillian of today.

She spent much time with Djuna.

Paul felt his mother removed in some way. He noticed that she and his father had little to say to each other. He was anxious. Adele had nightmares that her mother was dying. Larry was concerned. Perhaps Lillian was not well. She ate little. He sent for the doctor. She objected to him violently. Nanny hovered, guarded, as if she scented danger. But nothing changed. Lillian waited. She always went first to the kitchen when she came home, as if it were the hearth itself, to warm herself. An then to each child's room, and then to Larry.

She could do nothing. Djuna's words illuminated her chaos, but changed nothing. What was it Djuna said: that life tended to crystallize into patterns which became traps and webs. That people tended to see each other in their first "state" or "form" and to adopt a rhythm in consequence. That they had greatest difficulty in seeing the transformations of the loved one, in seeing the becoming. If they did finally perceive the new self, they had the greatest difficulty nevertheless in changing the rhythm. The strong one was condemned to perpetual strength, the weak to perpetual weakness. The one who loved you best condemned you to a static role because he had adapted his being to the past self. If you attempted to change, warned Djuna, you would find a subtle, perverse opposition, and perhaps sabotage! Inwardly and outwardly, a pattern was a form which became a prison. And then we had to smash it. Mutation was difficult. Attempts at evasion were frequent, blind evasions, evasions from dead relationships, false relationships, false roles, and sometimes from the deeper self too, because of the great obstacle one encountered in affirming it. All our emotional history was that of the spider and the fly, with the added tragedy that the fly here collaborated in the weaving of the web. Crimes were frequent. People in desperation turned about and destroyed each other. No one could detect the cause or catch the criminal. There was no visible victim. It always had the appearance of suicide.

Lillian sensed the walls and locks. She did not even know she wanted to escape. She did not even know she was in rebellion. She did it with her body. Her body became ill from the friction, lacerations and daily duels with her beloved jailers. Her body became ill from the poisons of internal rebellion, the monotony of her prison, the greyness of its days, the poverty of the nourishment. She was in a fixed relationship and could not move forward.

Anxiety settled upon the house. Paul clung to his mother longer when they separated for short periods. Adele was less gay.

Larry was more silent.

Nanny began to weep noiselessly. Then she had a visitor. The same one she had sent away ten years earlier. The man was growing old. He wanted a home. He wanted Nanny. Nanny was growing old. He talked to her all evening, in the kitchen. Then one day Nanny cried without control. Lillian questioned her. She wanted to get married. But she hated to leave the family. The family! The sacred, united, complete family. In this big house, with so much work. And no one else to be had. And she wanted Lillian to protest, to cling to her — as the children did before, as Larry had done a few years back, each time the suitor had come again for his answer. But Lillian said quietly, "Nanny, it is time that you thought of yourself.

You have lived for others all your life. Get married. I believe you should get married. He loves you. He waited for you such a long time. You deserve a home and life and protection and a rest. Get married."

And then Lillian walked into the dining room where the family was eating and she said: "Nanny is going to get married and leave us."

Paul then cried out: "This is the beginning of the end!"

Larry looked up from his meal, for the first time struck with a clearer glimpse of what had been haunting the house.

⁘

Through the high building, the wind complained, playing a frenzied flute up and down the elevator shafts.

Lillian and Djuna opened the window and looked at the city covered with a mist. One could see only the lighted eyes of the buildings. One could hear only muffled sounds, the ducks from Central Park lake nagging loudly, the fog horns from the river which sounded at times like the mournful complaints of imprisoned ships not allowed to sail, at others like gay departures.

Lillian was sitting in the dark, speaking of her life, her voice charged with both laughter and tears.

In the dark a new being appears. A new being who has not the courage to face daylight. In the dark people dare to dream everything. And they dare to tell everything. In the dark there appeared a new Lillian.

There was just enough light from the city to show their faces chalk white, with shadows in the place of eyes and mouth, and an occasional gleam of white teeth. At first it was like two children sitting on a see-saw, because Lillian would talk about her life and her marriage and the disintegration of her home, and then Djuna would lean over to embrace her, overflowing with pity. Then Djuna would speak and Lillian would lean over and want to gather her in her arms with maternal compassion.

"I feel," said Lillian, "that I do everything wrong. I feel I do everything to bring about just what I fear. You will turn away from me too."

Lillian's unsatisfied hunger for life had evoked in Djuna another hunger. This hunger still hovered at times over the bright film of her eyes, shading them not with the violet shadows of either illness or sensual excess, of experience or fever, but with the pearl-grey shadow of denial, and Djuna said:

"I was born in the most utter poverty. My mother lying in bed with consumption, four brothers and sisters loudly claiming food and care, and I having to be the mother and nurse of them all. We were so hungry that we ate all the samples of food or medicines which were left at the house. I remember once we ate a whole box of chocolate-coated constipation pills. Father was a taxi driver but he spent the greatest part of what he made on drink along the way. As we lived among people who were all living as we were, without sufficient clothing, or heat or food, we knew no contrast and believed this was natural and general. But with me it was different. I suffered from other kinds of pangs. I was prone to the most excessive dreaming, of such intensity and realism that when I awakened I felt I lost an entire universe of legends, myths, figures and cities of such color that they made our room seem a thousand times more bare, the poverty of the table more acute. The disproportion was immense. And I'm not speaking merely of the banquets which were so obviously compensatory! Nor of the obvious way by which I filled my poor wardrobe. It was more than that. I saw in my dreams houses, forests, entire cities, and such a variety of personages that even today I wonder how a child, who had not even seen pictures, could invent such designs in textures, such colonnades, friezes, fabulous animals, statues, colors, as I did. And the activity! My dreams were so full of activity that at times I felt it was the dreams which exhausted me rather than all the washing, ironing, shopping, mending, sweeping, tending, nursing, dusting that I did. I remember I had to break soap boxes to burn in the fireplace. I used to scratch my hands and bruise my toes. Yet when my mother caressed me and said, you look tired, Djuna, I almost felt like confessing to her that what had tired me was my constant dreaming of a ship which insisted on sailing through a city, or my voyage in a chaise through the snow-covered steppes of Russia. And by the way, there was a lot of confusion of places and methods of travel in my dreams, as there must be in the dreams of the blind. Do you know what I think now? I think what tired me was the intensity of the pleasures I had together with the perfect awareness that such pleasure could not last and would be immediately followed by its opposite. Once out of my dreams, the only certitude I retained from these nocturnal expeditions was that pleasure could not possibly last. This conviction was strengthened by the fact that no matter how small a pleasure I wanted to take during the day it was followed by catastrophe. If I relaxed for one instant the watch over my sick mother to eat an orange all by myself in some abandoned lot, she would have a turn for the worse. Or if I spent some time looking at the pictures outside of the movie house one of my brothers or sisters would cut himself or burn his finger or get into a fight with another child. So I felt then that liberty must be paid for heavily. I learned a most severe accounting which was to consider pleasure as the jewel, a kind of stolen jewel for which one must be willing to pay vast sums in suffering and guilt. Even today, Lillian, when something very marvellous happens to me, when I attain love or ecstasy or a perfect moment, I expect it to be followed by pain."

Then Lillian leaned over and kissed Djuna warmly: "I want to protect you."

"We give each other courage."

The mist came into the room. Djuna thought: She's such a hurt woman. She is one who does not know what she suffers from, or why, or how to overcome it. She is all unconscious, motion, music. She is afraid to see, to analyze her nature. She thinks that nature just is and that nothing can be done about it. She would never have invented ships to conquer the sea, machines to create light where there was darkness. She would never have harnessed water power, electric power. She is like the primitive. She thinks it is all beyond her power. She accepts chaos. She suffers mutely. . . .

"Djuna, tell me all that happened to you. I keep thinking about your hunger. I feel the pangs of it in my own stomach."

"My mother died," continued Djuna, "one of my brothers was hurt in an accident while playing in the street and crippled. Another was taken to the insane asylum. He harmed nobody. When the war started he began to eat flowers stolen from the florists. When he was arrested he said that he was eating flowers to bring peace to the world. That if everybody ate flowers peace would come to the world. My sister and I were put in an orphan asylum. I remember the day we were taken there. The night before I had a dream about a Chinese pagoda all in gold, filled with a marvelous odor. At the tip of the pagoda there was a mechanical bird who sang one little song repeatedly. I kept hearing this song and smelling the odor all the time and that seemed more real to me than the callous hands of the orphan asylum women when they changed me into a uniform. Oh, the greyness of those dresses! And if only the windows had been normal. But they were long and narrow, Lillian. Everything is changed when you look at it through long and narrow windows. It's as if the sky itself were compressed, limited. To me they were like the windows of a prison. The food was dark, and tasteless, like slime. The children were cruel to each other. No one visited us. And then there was the old watchman who made the rounds at night. He often lifted the corners of our bedcovers, and let his eyes rove and sometimes more than his eyes. . . . He became the demon of the night for us little girls."

There was a silence, during which both Lillian and Djuna became children, listening to the watchman of the night become the demon of the night, the tutor of the forbidden, the initiator breaking the sheltered core of the child, breaking the innocence and staining the beds of adolescence.

"The satyr of the asylum," said Djuna, "who became also our jailer because when we grew older and wanted to slip out at night to go out with the boys, it was he who rattled the keys and prevented us. But for him we might have been free at times, but he watched us, and the women looked up to him for his fanaticism in keeping us from the street. The orphan asylum had a system which permitted families to adopt the orphans. But as it was known that the asylum supplied the sum of thirty-five dollars a month towards the feeding of the child, those who responded were most often those in need of the thirty-five dollars. Poor families, already burdened with many children, came forward to 'adopt' new ones. The orphans were allowed to enter these homes in which they found themselves doubly cheated. For at least in the asylum we had no illusion, no hope of love. But we did have illusions about the adoptions. We thought we would find a family. In most cases we did not even imagine that these families had children of their own. We expected to be a much wanted and only child! I was placed in one of them. The first thing that happened was that the other children were jealous of the intruder. And the spectacle of the love lavished on the legitimate children was terribly painful. It made me feel more abandoned, more hungry, more orphaned than ever. Every time a parent embraced his child I suffered so much that finally I ran away back to the asylum. And I was not the only one. And besides this emotional starvation we got even less to eat – the allowance being spent on the whole family. And now I lost my last treasure: the dreaming. For nothing in the dreams took the place of the human warmth I had witnessed. Now I felt utterly poor, because I could not create a human companion."

This hunger which had inhabited her entire being, which had thinned her blood, transpired through her bones, attacked the roots of her hair, given a fragility to her skin which was never to disappear entirely, had been so enormous that it had marked her whole being and her eyes with an indelible mark. Although her life changed and every want was filled later, this appearance of hunger remained. As if nothing could ever quite fill it. Her being had received no sun, no food, no air, no warmth, no love. It retained open pores of yearning and longing, mysterious spongy cells of absorption. The space between actuality, absolute deprivation, and the sumptuosity of her imagination could never be entirely covered. What she had created in the void, in the emptiness, in the bareness continued to shame all that was offered her, and her large, infinitely blue eyes continued to assert the immensity of her hunger.

This hunger of the eyes, skin, of the whole body and spirit, which made others criminals, robbers, rapers, barbarians, which caused wars, invasions, plundering and murder, in Djuna at the age of puberty alchemized into love.

Whatever was missing she became: she became mother, father, cousin, brother, friend, confidant, guide, companion to all.

This power of absorption, this sponge of receptivity which might have fed itself forever to fill the early want, she used to receive all communication of the need of others. The need and hunger became nourishment. Her breasts, which no poverty had been able to wither, were heavy with the milk of lucidity, the milk of devotion.

This hunger . . . became love.

While wearing the costume of utter feminity, the veils and the combs, the gloves and the perfumes, the muffs and the heels of femininity, she nevertheless disguised in herself an active lover of the world, the one who was actively roused by the object of his love, the one who was made strong as man is made strong in the center of his being by the softness of his love. Loving in men and women not their strength but their softness, not their fullness but their hunger, not their plenitude but their needs.

⁘

They had made contact then with the deepest aspect of themselves—Djuna with Lillian's emotional violence and her compassion for this force which destroyed her and hurled her against all obstacles, Lillian with Djuna's power of clarification. They needed each other. Djuna experienced deep in herself a pleasure each time Lillian exploded, for she herself kept her gestures, her feeling within an outer form, like an Oriental. When Lillian exploded it seemed to Djuna as if some of her violent feeling, so long contained within the forms, were released. Some of her own lightning, some of her own rebellions, some of her own angers. Djuna contained in herself a Lillian too, to whom she had never given a moment's freedom, and it made her strangely free when Lillian gave vent to her anger or rebellions. But after the havoc, when Lillian had bruised herself, or more seriously mutilated herself (war and explosion had their consequences) then Lilian needed Djuna. For the bitterness, the despair, the chaos submerged Lillian, drowned her. The hurt Lillian wanted to strike back and did so blindly, hurting herself all the more. And then Djuna was there, to remove the arrows implanted in Lillian, to cleanse them of their poison, to open the prison door, to open the trap door, to protect, to give transfusion of blood, and peace to the wounded.

But it was Lillian who was drowning, and it was Djuna who was able always at the last moment to save her, and in her moments of danger, Lilian knew only one thing: that she must possess Djuna.

It was as if someone had proclaimed: I need oxygen, and therefore I will lock some oxygen in my room and live on it.

So Lillian began her courtship.

She brought gifts. She pulled out perfume, and jewelry and clothes. She almost covered the bed with gifts. She wanted Djuna to put all the jewelry on, to smell all the perfumes at once, to wear all her clothes. Djuna was showered with gifts as in a fairytale, but she could not find in them the fairytale pleasure. She felt that to each gift was tied a little invisible cord or demand, of exactingness, of debt, of domination. She felt she could not wear all these things and walk away, freely. She felt that with the gifts, a golden spider wove a golden web of possession. Lillian was not only giving away objects, but golden threads woven out of her very own substance to fix and to hold. They were not the fairytale gifts which Djuna had dreamed of receiving. (She had many dreams of receiving perfume, or receiving fur, or being given blue bottles, lamés, etc.) In the fairytale the giver laid out the presents and then became invisible. In the fairytales and in the dreams there was no debt, and there was no giver.

Lillian did not become invisible. Lillian became more and more present. Lillian became the mother who wanted to dress her child out of her own substance, Lillian became the lover who wanted to slip the shoes and slippers on the beloved's feet so he could contain these feet. The dresses were not chosen as Djuna's dresses, but as Lillian's choice and taste to cover Djuna.

The night of gifts, begun in gayety and magnificence, began to thicken. Lillian had put too much of herself into the gifts. It was a lovely night, with the gifts scattered through the room like fragments of Miro's circus paintings, flickering and leaping, but not free. Djuna wanted to enjoy and she could not. She loved Lillian's generosity, Lillian's largeness, Lillian's opulence and magnificence, but she felt anxiety. She remembered as a child receiving gifts for Christmas, and among them a closed mysterious box gayly festooned with multicolored ribbons. She remembered that the mystery of this box affected her more than the open, exposed, familiar gifts of tea cups, dolls, etc. She opened the box and out of it jumped a grotesque devil who, propelled by taut springs, almost hit her face.

In these gifts, there is a demon somewhere; a demon who is hurting Lillian, and will hurt me, and I don't know where he is hiding. I haven't seen him yet, but he is here.

She thought of the old legends, of the knights who had to kill monsters before they could enjoy their love.

No demon here, thought Djuna, nothing but a woman drowning, who is clutching at me . . . I love her.

When Lillian dressed up in the evening in vivid colors with her ever tinkling jewelry, her face wildly alive, Djuna said to her, "You're made for a passionate life of some kind."

She looked like a white negress, a body made for rolling in natural undulations of pleasure and desire. Her vivid face, her avid mouth, her provocative, teasing glances proclaimed sensuality. She had rings under her eyes. She looked often as if she had just come from the arms of a lover. An energy smoked from her whole body.

But sensuality was paralyzed in her. When Djuna sought to show her face of herself in the mirror, she found Lillian paralyzed with fear. She was impaled on a rigid pole of puritanism. One felt it, like a heavy silver chastity belt, around her soft, rounded body.

She bought a black lace gown like Djuna's. Then she wanted to own all the objects which carried Djuna's personality or spirit. She wanted to be clasped at the wrists by Djuna's bracelet watch, dressed in Djuna's kind of clothes.

(Djuna thought of the primitives eating the liver of the strong man of the tribe to acquire his strength, wearing the teeth of the elephant to acquire his durability, donning the lion's head and mane to appropriate his courage, gluing feathers on themselves to become as free as the bird.)

Lillian knew no mystery. Everything was open with her. Even the most ordinary mysteries of women she did not guard. She was open like a man, frank, direct. Her eyes shed lightning but no shadows.

⁘

One night Djuna and Lillian went to a night club together to watch the cancan. At such a moment Djuna forgot that she was a woman and looked at the women dancing with the eyes of an artist and the eyes of a man. She admired them, revelled in their beauty, in their seductions, in the interplay of black garters and black stockings and the snow-white frills of petticoats.

Lillian's face clouded. The storm gathered in her eyes. The lightning struck. She lashed out in anger: "If I were a man I would murder you."

Djuna was bewildered. Then Lillian's anger dissolved in lamentations: "Oh, the poor people, the poor people who love you. You love these women!"

She began to weep. Djuna put her arms around her and consoled her. The people around them looked baffled, as passers-by look up suddenly at an unexpected, freakish windstorm. Here it was, chaotically upsetting the universe, coming from right and left, great fury and velocity – and why?

Two women were looking at beautiful women dancing. One enjoyed it, and the other made a scene.

Lillian went home and wrote stuttering phrases on the back of a box of writing paper: Djuna, don't abandon me; if you abandon me, I am lost.

When Djuna came the next day, still angry from the inexplicable storm of the night before, she wanted to say: are you the woman I chose for a friend? Are you the egotistical, devouring child, all caprice and confusion who is always crossing my path? She could not say it, not before this chaotic helpless writing on the back of the box, a writing which could not stand alone, but wavered from left to right, from right to left, inclining, falling, spilling, retreating, ascending on the line as if for flight off the edge of the paper as if it were an airfield, or plummeting on the paper like a falling elevator.

If they met a couple along the street who were kissing, Lillian became equally unhinged.

If they talked about her children and Djuna said: I never liked real children, only the child in the grown-up, Lillian answered: you should have had children.

"But I lack the maternal feeling for children, Lillian, though I haven't lacked the maternal experience. There are plenty of children, abandoned children right in the so-called grown-ups. While you, well you are a real mother, you have a real maternal capacity. You are the mother type. I am not. I only like being the mistress. I don't even like being a wife."

Then Lillian's entire universe turned a somersault again, crashed, and Djuna was amazed to see the devastating results of an innocent phrase: "I am not a maternal woman," she said, as if it were an accusation. (Everything was an accusation.)

Then Djuna kissed her and said playfully: "Well, then, you're a femme fatale!"

But this was like fanning an already enormous flame. This aroused Lillian to despair: "No, no, I never destroyed or hurt anybody," she protested.

"You know, Lillian, someday I will sit down and write a little dictionary for you, a little Chinese dictionary. In it I will put down all the interpretations of what is said to you, the right interpretation, that is: the one that is not meant to injure, not meant to humiliate or accuse or doubt. And whenever something is said to you, you will look in my little dictionary to make sure, before you get desperate, that you have understood what is said to you."

The idea of the little Chinese dictionary made Lillian laugh. The storm passed.

But if they walked the streets together her obsession was to see who was looking at them or following them. In the shops she was obsessed about her plumpness and considered it not an attribute but a defect. In the movies it was emotionalism and tears. If they sat in a restaurant by a large window and saw the people passing it was denigration and dissection. The universe hinged and turned on her defeated self.

She was aggressive with people who waited on her, and then was hurt by their defensive abandon of her. When they did not wait on her she was personally injured, but could not see the injury she had inflicted by her demanding ways. Her commands bristled everyone's hair, raised obstacles and retaliations. As soon as she appeared she brought dissonance.

But she blamed the others, the world.

She could not bear to see lovers together, absorbed in each other.

She harassed the quiet men and lured them to an argument and she hated the aggressive men who held their own against her.

Her shame. She could not carry off gallantly a run in her stocking. She was overwhelmed by a lost button.

When Djuna was too swamped by other occupations or other people to pay attention to her, Lillian became ill. But she would not be ill at home surrounded by her family. She was ill alone, in a hotel room, so that Djuna ran in and out with medicines, with chicken soup, stayed with her day and night chained to her antics, and then Lillian clapped her hands and confessed: "I'm so happy! Now I've got you all to myself!"

The summer nights were passing outside like gay whores, with tinkles of cheap jewelry, opened and emollient like a vast bed. The summer nights were passing but not Lillian's tension with the world.

She read erotic memoirs avidly, she was obsessed with the lives and loves of others. But she herself could not yield, she was ashamed, she throttled her own nature, and all this desire, lust, became twisted inside of her and churned a poison of envy and jealousy. Whenever sensuality showed its flower head, Lillian would have liked to decapitate it, so it would cease troubling and haunting her.

At the same time she wanted to seduce the world, Djuna, everybody. She would want to be kissed on the lips and more warmly and then violently block herself. She thrived on this hysterical undercurrent without culmination. This throbbing sensual obsession and the blocking of it; this rapacious love without polarity, like a blind womb appetite; delighting in making the temperature rise and then clamping down the lid.

In her drowning she was like one constantly choking those around her, bringing them down with her into darkness.

Djuna felt caught in a sirocco.

She had lived once on a Spanish island and experienced exactly this impression.

The island had been calm, silvery and dormant until one morning when a strange wind began to blow from Africa, blowing in circles. It swept over the island charged with torpid warmth, charged with flower smells, with sandalwood and patchouli and incense, and turning in whirlpools, gathered up the nerves and swinging with them into whirlpools of dry enervating warmth and smells, reached no climax, no explosion. Blowing persistently, continuously, hour after hour, gathering every nerve in every human being, the nerves alone, and tangling them in this fatal waltz; drugging them and pulling them, and whirlpooling them, until the body shook with restlessness – all polarity and sense of gravity lost. Because of this insane waltz of the wind, its emollient warmth, its perfumes, the being lost its guidance, its clarity, its integrity. Hour after hour, all day and all night, the body was subjected to this insidious whirling rhythm, in which polarity was lost, and only the nerves and desires throbbed, tense and weary of movement – all in a void, with no respite, no climax, no great loosening as in other storms. A tension that gathered force but had no release. It abated not once in forty-eight hours, promising, arousing, caressing, destroying sleep, rest, repose, and then vanished without releasing, without culmination. . . .

This violence which Djuna had loved so much! It had become a mere sirocco wind, burning and shrivelling. This violence which Djuna had applauded, enjoyed, because she could not possess it in herself. It was now burning her, and their friendship. Because it was not attached to anything, it was not creating anything, it was a trap of negation.

"You will save me," said Lillian always, clinging.

Lillian was the large foundering ship, yes, and Djuna the small lifeboat. But now the big ship had been moored to the small lifeboat and was pitching too fast and furiously and the lifeboat was being swamped.

(She wants something of me that only a man can give her. But first of all she wants to become me, so that she can communicate with man. She has lost her ways of communicating with man. She is doing it through me!)

When they walked together, Lillian sometimes asked Djuna: "Walk in front of me, so I can see how you walk. You have such a sway of the hips!"

In front of Lillian walked Lillian's lost femininity, imprisoned in the male Lillian. Lillian's femininity imprisoned in the deepest wells of her being, loving Djuna, and knowing it must reach her own femininity at the bottom of the well by way of Djuna. By wearing Djuna's feminine exterior, swaying her hips, becoming Djuna.

As Djuna enjoyed Lillian's violence, Lillian enjoyed Djuna's feminine capitulations: The pleasure Djuna took in her capitulations to love, to desire. Lillian breathed out through Djuna. What took place in Djuna's being which Lillian could not reach, she at least reached by way of Djuna.

"The first time a boy hurt me," said Lillian to Djuna. "it was in school. I don't remember what he did. But I wept. And he laughed at me. Do you know what I did? I went home and dressed in my brother's suit. I tried to feel as the boy felt. Naturally as I put on the suit I felt I was putting on a costume of strength. It made me feel sure, as the boy was, confident, impudent. The mere fact of putting my hands in the pockets made me feel arrogant. I thought then that to be a boy meant one did not suffer. That it was being a girl that was responsible for the suffering. Later I felt the same way. I thought man had found a way out of suffering by objectivity. What the man called being reasonable. When my husband said: Lillian, let's be reasonable, it meant he had none of the feeling I had, that he could be objective. What a power! Then there was another thing. When I felt his great choking anguish I discovered one relief, and that was action. I felt like the women who had to sit and wait at home while there was a war going on. I felt if only I could join the war, participate, I wouldn't feel the anguish and the fear. All through the last war as a child I felt: if only they would let me be Joan of Arc. Joan of Arc wore a suit of armor, she sat on a horse, she fought side by side with the men. She must have gained their strength. Then it was the same way about men. At a dance, as a girl, the moment of waiting before they asked me seemed intolerable, the suspense, and the insecurity; perhaps they were not going to ask me! So I rushed forward, to cut the suspense. I rushed. All my nature became rushed, propelled by the anxiety, merely to cut through all the moment of anxious uncertainty."

Djuna looked tenderly at her, not the strong Lillian, the overwhelming Lillian, the aggressive Lillian, but the hidden, secret, frightened Lillian who had created such a hard armor and disguise around her weakness.

Djuna saw the Lillian hidden in her coat of armor, and all of Lillian's armor lay broken around her, like cruel pieces of mail which had wounded her more than they had protected her from the enemy. The mail had melted, and revealed the bruised feminine flesh. At the first knowledge of the weakness Lillian had picked up the mail, wrapped herself in it and had taken up a lance. The lance! The man's lance. Uncertainty resolved, relieved by the activity of attack!

The body of Lillian changed as she talked, the fast coming words accelerating the dismantling. She was taking off the shell, the covering, the defenses, the coat of mail, the activity.

Suddenly Lillian laughed. In the middle of tears, she laughed: "I'm remembering a very comical incident. I was about sixteen. There was a boy in love with me. Shyly, quietly in love. We were in the same school but he lived quite far away. We all used bicycles. One day we were going to be separated for a week by the holidays. He suggested we both bicycle together towards a meeting place between the two towns. The week of separation seemed too unbearable. So it was agreed: at a certain hour we would leave the house together and meet half way."

Lillian started off. At first at a normal pace. She knew the rhythm of the boy. A rather easy, relaxed rhythm. Never rushed. Never precipitate. She at first adopted his rhythm. Dreaming of him, of his slow smile, of his shy worship, of his expression of this worship, which consisted mainly in waiting for her here, there. Waiting. Not advancing, inviting, but waiting. Watching her pass by.

She pedaled slowly, dreamily. Then slowly her pleasure and tranquility turned to anguish: suppose he did not come? Suppose she arrived before him? Could she bear the sight of the desolate place of their meeting, the failed meeting? The exaltation that had been increasing in her, like some powerful motor, what could she do with this exaltation if she arrived alone, and the meeting failed? The fear affected her in two directions. She could stop right there, and turn back, and not face the possibility of disappointment, or she could rush forward and accelerate the moment of painful suspense, and she chose the second. Her lack of confidence in life, in realization, in the fufillment of her desires, in the outcome of a dream, in the possibility of reality corresponding to her fantasy, speeded her bicycle with the incredible speed of anxiety, a speed beyond the human body, beyond human endurance.

She arrived before him. Her fear was justified! She could not measure what the anxiety had done to her speed, the acceleration which had broken the equality of rhythm. She arrived as she had feared, at a desolate spot on the road, and the boy had become this invisible image which taunts the dreamer, a mirage that could not be made real. It had become reality eluding the dreamer, the wish unfulfilled.

The boy may have arrived later. He may have fallen asleep and not come at all. He may have had a tire pucture. Nothing mattered. Nothing could prevent her from feeling that she was not Juliet waiting on the balcony, but Romeo who had to leap across space to join her. She had leaped, she had acted Romeo, and when woman leaped she leaped into a void.

Later it was not the drama of two bicycles, of a road, of two separated towns; later it was a darkened room, and a man and woman pursuing pleasure and fusion.

At first she lay passive dreaming of the pleasure that would come out of the darkness, to dissolve and invade her. But it was not pleasure which came out of the darkness to clasp her. It was anxiety. Anxiety made confused gestures in the dark, crosscurrents of forces, short circuits, and no pleasure. A depression, a broken rhythm, a feeling such as men must have after they have taken a whore.

Out of the prone figure of the woman, apparently passive, apparently receptive, there rose a taut and anxious shadow, the shadow of the woman bicycling too fast; who, to relieve her insecurity, plunges forward as the desperado does and is defeated because this aggressiveness cannot meet its mate and unite with it. A part of the woman has not participated in this marriage, has not been taken. But was it a part of the woman, or the shadow of anxiety, which dressed itself in man's clothes and assumed man's active role to quiet its anguish? Wasn't it the woman who dressed as a man and pedalled too fast?

⁘

Jay. The table at which he sat was stained with wine. His blue eyes were inscrutable like those of a Chinese sage. He ended all his phrases in a kind of hum, as if he put his foot on the pedal of his voice and created an echo. In this way none of his phrases ended abruptly.

Sitting at the bar he immediately created a climate, a tropical day. In spite of the tension in her, Lillian felt it. Sitting at a bar with his voice rolling over, he dissolved and liquefied the hard click of silver on plates, the icy dissonances of glasses, the brittle sound of money thrown on the counter.

He was tall but he carried his tallness slackly and easily, as easily as his coat and hat, as if all of it could be discarded and sloughed off at any moment when he needed lightness or nimbleness. His body large, shaggy, as if never definitely chiselled, never quite ultimately finished, was as casually his as his passing moods and varying fancies and fortunes.

He opened his soft animal mouth a little, as if in expectancy of a drink. But instead, he said (as if he had absorbed Lillian's face and voice in place of the drink), "I'm happy. I'm too happy." Then he began to laugh, to laugh, to laugh, with his head shaking like a bear, shaking from right to left as if it were too heavy a head. "I can't help it. I can't help laughing. I'm too happy. Last night I spent the night here. It was Christmas and I didn't have the money for a hotel room. And the night before I slept at a movie house. They overlooked me, didn't sweep where I lay. In the morning I played the movie piano. In walked the furious manager, then he listened, then he gave me a contract starting this evening. Christ, Lillian, I never thought Christmas would bring me anything, yet it brought you."

How gently he had walked into her life, how quietly he seemed to be living, while all the time he was drawing bitter caricatures on the bar table, on the backs of envelope. Drawing bums, drunks, derelicts.

"So you're a pianist . . . that's what I should have been. I'm not bad, but I would never work hard enough. I wanted also to be a painter. I might have been a writer too, if I had worked enough. I did a bit of acting too, at one time. As it is, I guess I'm the last man on earth. Why did you single me out?"

This man who would not be distinguished in a crowd, who

could pass through it like an ordinary man, so quiet, so absorbed, with his hat on one side, his steps dragging a little, like a lazy devil enjoying everything, why did she see him hungry, thirsty, abandoned?

Behind this Jay, with his southern roguishness, perpetually calling for drinks, why did she see a lost man?

He sat like a workman before his drinks, he talked like a cart driver to the whores at the bar; they were all at ease with him. His presence took all the straining and willing out of Lillian. He was like the south wind: blowing when he came, melting and softening, bearing joy and abundance.

When they met, and she saw him walking towards her, she felt he would never stop walking towards her and into her very being: he would walk right into her being with his soft lazy walk and purring voice and his mouth slightly open.

She could not hear his voice. His voice rumbled over the surface of her skin, like another caress. She had no power against his voice. It came straight from him into her. She could stuff her ears and still it would find its way into her blood and make it rise.

All things were born anew when her dress fell on the floor of his room.

He said: "I feel humble, Lillian, but it is all so good, so good." He gave to the word good a mellowness which made the whole room glow, which gave a warmer color to the bare window, to the woollen shirt hung on a peg, to the single glass out of which they drank together.

Behind the yellow curtain the sun seeped in: everything was the color of a tropical afternoon.

The small room was like a deep-set alcove. Warm mist and

warm blood; the high drunkenness which made Jay flushed and heavy blooded. His sensual features expanded.

"As soon as you come, I'm jubilant." And he did somersaults on the bed, two or three of them.

"This is fine wine, Lillian. Let's drink to my failure. There's no doubt about it, no doubt whatever that I'm a failure."

"I won't let you be a failure," said Lillian.

"You say: I want, as if that made things happen."

"It does."

"I don't know what I expect of you. I expect miracles." He looked up at her slyly, then mockingly, then gravely again. "I have no illusions," he said.

Then he sat down with his heavy shoulders bowed, and his head bowed, but Lillian caught that swift, passing flash, a moment's hope, the lightning passage of a spark of faith left in his indifference to his fate. She clung to this.

⁘

Jay — gnome and sprite and faun, and playboy of the motherbound world. Brightly gifted, he painted while he enjoyed the painting; the accidental marvels of colors, the pleasant shock of apparitions made in a game with paint. He stopped painting where the effort began, the need for discipline or travail. He danced while he was allowed to improvise, to surprise himself and others, to stretch, laugh, and court and be courted; but stopped if there were studying, developing or disciplining or effort or repetition involved. He acted, he acted loosely, flowingly, emotionally, while nothing more difficult was demanded of him, but he evaded rehearsals, fatigue, strain, effort. He pursued no friend, he took what came.

He gave himself to the present moment. To be with the friend, to drink with the friend, to talk with the friend, he forgot what was due the next day, and if it were something which demanded time, or energy, he could not meet it. He had not provided for it. He was asleep when he should have been awake, and tired when his energy was required, and absent when his presence was summoned. The merest expectation from a friend, the most trivial obligation, sent him running in the opposite direction. He came to the friend while there was pleasure to be had. He left as soon as the pleasure vanished and reality began. An accident, an illness, poverty, a quarrel – he was never there for them.

It was as if he smelled the climate: was it good? Was there the odor of pleasure, the colors of pleasure? Expansion, forgetfulness, abandon, enjoyment? They he stayed. Difficulties? Then he vanished.

⁂

Lillian and Jay.

It was a merciless winter day. The wind persecuted them around the corners of the street. The snow slid into their collars. They could not talk to each other. They took a taxi.

The windows of the taxi had frosted, so they seemed completely shut off from the rest of the world. It was small and dark and warm. Jay buried his face in her fur. He made himself small. He had a way of becoming so passive and soft that he seemed to lose his height and weight. He did this now, his face in her fur, and she felt as if she were the darkness, the smallness of the taxi, and were hiding him, protecting him from the elements. Here the cold could not reach him, the snow, the wind, the daylight. He sheltered himself, she carried his head on her breast, she carried his body become limp, his hands nestling in her pocket. She was the fur, the pocket, the warmth that sheltered him. She felt immense, and strong, and illimitable, the boundless mother opening her arms and her wings, flying to carry him somewhere; she his shelter and refuge, his secret hiding place, his tent, his sky, his blanket.

The soundproof mother, the shockproof mother of man!

This passion warmer, stronger than the other passion, annihilating desire and becoming the desire, a boundless passion to surround, envelop, sustain, strengthen, uphold, to answer all needs. He closed his eyes. He almost slept in her warmth and furriness. He caressed the fur, he feared no claws, he abandoned himself, and the waves of passion inspired by his abandon intoxicated her.

⁘

He usually wore colored shirts to suit his fancy. Once he wore a white one, because it had been given to him. It did not suit him. Whiteness and blackness did not suit him. Only the intermediate colors.

Lillian was standing near him and they had just been discussing their life together. Jay had admitted that he would not work. He could not bear repetition, he could not bear a "boss," he could not bear regular hours. He could not bear the seriousness.

"Then you will have to be a hobo."

"I'll be a hobo, then."

"A hobo has no wife," said Lillian.

"No," he said. And added nothing. If she became part of the effort, he would not cling to her either.

"I will have to work, then," she said. "One of us has to work."

He said nothing.

Lillian was doubly disturbed by the unfamiliarity of the scene, the portentousness of it, and by the familiarity of the white shirt. The white shirt disturbed her more than his words. And then she knew. The white shirt reminded her of her husband. Just before he put on his coat she had always seen him and obscurely felt: how straight and rigid he stands in his white shirt. Black and white. Definite and starched, and always the same. But there it was. She was not sure she had liked the white shirt. From it came authority, a firm guidance, a firm construction. And now she was again facing a white shirt but with a strange feeling that there was nothing in it: no rigidity, no straight shoulders, no man. If she approached she would feel something fragile, soft and wavering: the shirt was not upheld by the body of the man. If she broke suddenly at the idea of assuming the responsibility, if she broke against this shirt it would collapse, turn to sand, trickle sand and soft laughter and elusive flickering love.

Against this white shirt of the husband she had lain her head once and heard a strong heart beat evenly, and now it was as if it were empty, and she were in a dream of falling down soft sand dunes to softer and more sliding shifty sand dunes. . . . Her head turned.

She kept herself on this new equilibrium by a great effort, fearing to touch the white shirt of weakness and to feel the yielding, the softness and the sand.

∴

When she sewed on buttons for him she was sewing not only buttons but also sewing together the sparse, disconnected fragments of his ideas, of his inventions, of his unfinished dreams. She was weaving and sewing and mending because he carried in himself no thread of connection, no knowledge of mending, no thread of continuity or repair. If he allowed a word to pass that was poisoned like a primitive arrow, he never sought the counter-poison, he never measured its fatal consequences. She was sewing on a button and the broken pieces of his waywardness; sewing a button and his words too loosely strung; sewing their days together to make a tapestry; their words together, their moods together, which he dispersed and tore. As he tore his clothes with his precipitations towards his wishes, his wanderings, his rambles, his peripheral journeys. She was sewing together the little proofs of his devotion out of which to make a garment for her tattered love and faith. He cut into the faith with negligent scissors, and she mended and sewed and rewove and patched. He wasted, and threw away, and could not evaluate or preserve, or contain, or keep his treasures. Like his ever torn pockets, everything slipped through and was lost, as he lost gifts, mementos—all the objects from the past. She sewed his pockets that he might keep some of their days together, hold together the key to the house, to their room, to their bed. She sewed the sleeve so he could reach out his arm and hold her, when loneliness dissolved her. She sewed the lining so that the warmth would not seep out of their days together, the soft inner skin of their relationship.

He always admitted and conceded to his own wishes first, before she admitted hers. Because he was sleepy, she had to become the panoply on which he rested. Her love must fan him if he were warm and be the fire if he were cold. In illness he required day and night nursing, one for the illness, the other for the pleasure he took in her attentiveness.

His helplessness made him the "*homme fatal*" for such a woman. He reached without sureness or nimbleness for the cup, for the food. Her hand flew to finish off the uncertain gesture, to supply the missing object. His hunger for anything metamorphosed her into an Aladdin's lamp: even his dreams must be fulfilled.

Towards the greater obstacles he assumed a definitely noncombatant attitude. Rather than claim his due, or face an angry landlord, or obtain a rightful privilege, his first impulse was to surrender. Move out of the house that could not be repaired, move out of the country if his papers were not in order, move out of a woman's way if another man stalked too near. Retreat, surrender.

⁘

At times Lillian remembered her husband, and now that he was no longer the husband she could see that he had been, as much as the other men she liked; handsome and desirable, and she could not understand why he had never been able to enter her being and her feelings as a lover. She had truly liked every aspect of him except the aspect of lover. When she saw him, with the clarity of distance and separation, she saw him quite outside of herself. He stood erect, and self-sufficient, and manly. He always retained his normal male largeness and upstanding protectiveness.

But Jay . . . came towards her almost as a man who limps and whom one instinctively wishes to sustain. He came as the man who did not see very well, slightly awkward, slightly stumbling. In this helplessness, in spite of his actual stature (he was the same height as her husband) he gave the air of being smaller, more fragile, more vulnerable. It was this fear in the man, who seemed inadequate in regard to life, trapped in it, the victim of it, which somehow affected her. In a smaller, weaker dimension he seemed to reach the right proportion for his being to enter into hers. He entered by the route of her compassion. She opened as the refuge opens; not conscious that it was a man who entered (man of whom she had a certain suspicion) but a child in need. Because he knocked as a beggar begging for a retreat, as a victim seeking solace, as a weakling seeking sustenance, she opened the door without suspicion.

It was in her frenzy to shelter, cover, defend him that she laid her strength over his head like an enormous starry roof, and the stretching immensity of the boundless mother was substituted for the normal image of the man covering the woman.

÷

Jay came and he had a cold. And though he at first pretended it was of no importance, he slowly melted entirely into her, became soft and tender, waiting to be pampered, exaggerating his cough. And they wandered through the city like two lazy southerners, he said, like two convalescents. And she pampered him laughingly, ignoring time, eating when they were hungry, and seeing a radium sunlight lighting up the rain, seeing only the shimmer of the wet streets and not the greyness. He confessed that he craved a phonograph, and they shopped together and brought it back in a taxi. They slept soundly inside the warmth of this closeness, in the luxury of their contentment. It was Jay who touched everything with the magic of his contentment. It was Jay who said: isn't this ham good, isn't this salad good, isn't this wine good. Everything was good and savory, palatable and expansive.

He gave her the savor of the present, and let her care for the morrow.

This moment of utter and absolute tasting of food, of color, this moment of human breathing. No fragment detached, errant, disconnected or lost. Because as Jay gathered the food on the table, the phonograph to his room, he gathered her into the present moment.

His taking her was not to take her or master her. He was the lover inside of the woman, as the child is inside of the woman. His caresses were as if he yearned and craved to be taken in not only as a lover; not merely to satisfy his desire but to remain within her. And her yearning answered this, by her desire to be filled. She never felt him outside of herself. Her husband had stood outside of her, and had come to visit her as a man, sensually. But he had not lodged himself as Jay had done, by reposing in her, by losing himself in her, by melting within her, with such feeling of physical intermingling as she had had with her child. Her husband had come to be renewed, to emerge again, to leave her and go to his male activities, to his struggles with the world.

The maternal and the feminine cravings were all confused in her, and all she felt was that it was through this softening and through this maternal yieldingness that Jay had penetrated where she had not allowed her husband's manliness to enter, only to visit her.

He liked prostitutes. "Because one does not have to make love to them, one does not have to write them beautiful letters." He liked them, and he liked to tell Lillian how much he liked them. He had to share all this with Lillian. He could not conceal any part of it from her, even if it hurt her. He could retain and hold nothing back from her. She was his confessor and his companion, his collaborator and his guardian angel. He did not see her weep when he launched into descriptions. At this moment he treated her as if she were a man (or the mother). As if the spectacle of his life could amuse her. "I even think if you had seen me that time, you could have enjoyed it."

He liked her to assume the burden of their life together, its material basis. Yet when she came to him, she must be all ready to discard this mantle of responsibilities, and became a child with him. His sense of humor took wayward forms.

His favorite prank: something that could be thrown away, which others valued; something that could be broken which others preserved. Traditions, habits, possessions. His greatest enjoyment was in demolition.

One of his most joyous experiences had been when a neighbor pianist who lived in the same quiet little street with him many years ago had been obliged to visit his mother at the hospital on the same day as the piano house had promised him an exchange

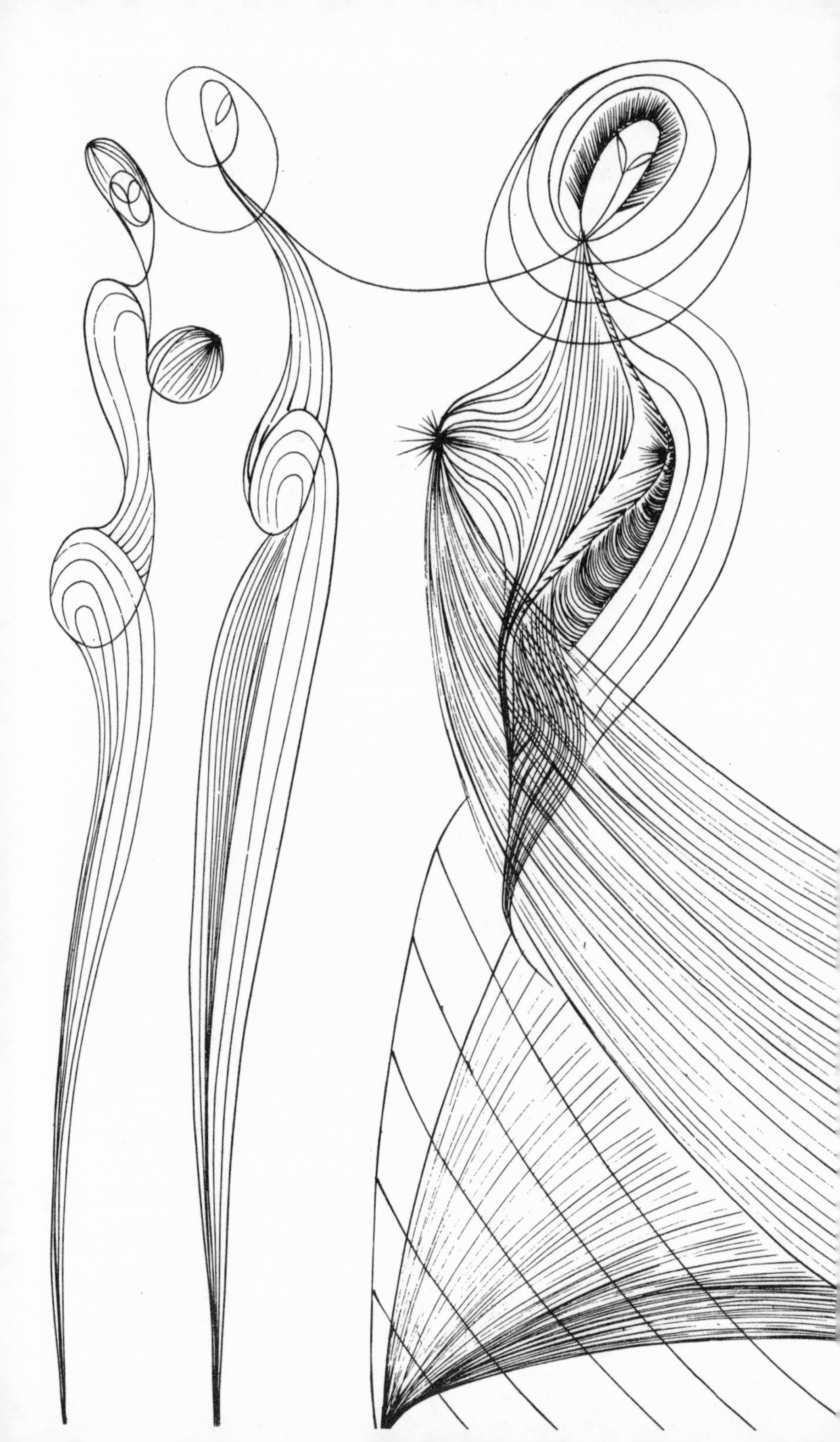

of pianos. The man had been looking forward to this for many months. He begged Jay to attend to this. It was a complicated affair, getting the old piano out and the new one in. It was to be done by two different houses. One, a moving man, was to take the old piano out, then the piano house was to deliver the new. Jay had laughed it all off, and walked out unconcernedly, never remembering the promise he made. When he came home he found the two pianos in the street, before the entrance of the house, and the rain pouring down on them. The sight of the two pianos in the rain sent him into an absolute state of gayety. "It was the most surrealistic sight I have ever seen in New York City." His laughter was so contagious that Lillian laughed with him, at the same time as she felt, somehow, a kind of pain at the image of pianos drenched in rain, and a pain even for the unknown pianist's feeling on his return home.

He seized only upon the comedy of the events.

At times Lillian asked herself: what will he make of me some day, when will he hurt me? And what if he does: I will try to love him gayly, more easily and loosely. To endure space and distance and betrayals. My courage is born today. Here lies Jay, breathing into my hair, over my neck. No hurt will come from me. No judgment. No woman ever judged the life stirring within her womb. I am too close to you. I will laugh with you even if it is against me.

Against me. Now the pain about the pianos left out in the rain suddenly touched her personally, and she understood why she had not been able to laugh freely. Those pianos were not only those of Jay's friend in the past, but her own too, since she had given up playing in order to work for Jay's support. She had surrendered any hope of becoming a concert pianist to attend better to their immediate needs. Jay's mockery wounded her, for it exposed his insensitiveness to anyone's loss, and to her loss too, his incapacity to feel for others, to understand that with the loss of her pianist self she had lost a very large part of herself, annihilated an entire portion of her personality, sacrificed it to him.

It was her piano Jay had left out in the rain, to be ruined. . . .

⁘

He was wearing bedroom slippers and he was painting, with a bottle of red wine beside him. Circles of red wine on the floor. Stains. The edge of the table was burnt by cigarette stubs.

He didn't care. He said that what he had painted today was not as good as yesterday, but he didn't care. He was enjoying it just the same. He wasn't worrying about art. Everything was good, hang perfection, and he was out of cigarettes and if she would give him one he might finish that water color. She had come to interrupt him, that was good too, that was life; life was more important than any painting, let the interruptions come, specially in the form of a woman; let people walk in, it was good, to paint was good, not to paint was just as good, and eating and love making were even better, and now he was finished and he was hungry, and he wished they might go to the movies, good or bad. . . .

The room was black. Jay was asleep in her arms, now, heavily asleep. She heard the organ grinder grinding his music. It was Saturday night. Always a holiday with him, always Saturday night with the crowds laughing and shouting and the organ grinder playing.

"According to the Chinese," said Jay, awakening, "there was a realm between heaven and earth . . . this must be it."

Tornadoes of desire and exquisite calms. She felt heavy and burnt.

"I want to keep you under lock and key, Lillian."

Suddenly he leaped up with a whiplike alacrity and exuberance and began to talk about his childhood, about his life in the streets, about the women he had loved and ditched, and the women who had ditched and bitched him, as he put it. He seemed to remember everything at once, as though it was a ball inside of him which unravelled of itself, and as it unravelled made new balls which he would unravel again another day. Had he actually done all these things he was relating to Lillian with such kaleidoscopic fury and passion? Had he really killed a boy in school with a snow ball? Had he really struck his first wife down when she was with child? Had he really butted his head against a wall in sudden anger because the woman he loved had rejected him? Had he really taken abortions and thrown them off the ferry boat in order to pick up a little extra change? Had he really stolen silver from a blind news vendor?

All the layers of his past he unravelled and laid before her, his masks, his buffooneries, and she saw him pretending, driven by obscure revenges, by fears, by weaknesses.

She saw him in the past and in the world, another man from the one she knew. And like all women in love she discarded this man of the past, holding others responsible for his behaviour; and thinking: before me he sheds all his poses and defences. The legend of hardness and callousness she did not believe. She saw him innocent, as we always see the loved one, innocent and even a victim.

She felt that she knew which was the rind and which the core of the man. "You always know," he said, "what is to be laughed away."

Then he rolled over and fell asleep. No noise, no care, no work undone, no imperfection unmastered, no love scene unresumed, no problem unsolved, ever kept him awake. He could roll over and forget. He could roll over with such grand indifference and let everything wait. When he rolled over the day ended. Nothing could be carried over into the next day. The next day would be absolutely new and clean. He just rolled over and extinguished everything. Just rolling over.

⁘

Djuna and Jay. For Djuna Jay does not look nonchalant but rather intent and listening, as if in quest of some revelation, as if he were questioning for the first time.

"I've lived so blindly. . . . No time to think much. Tons and tons of experience. Lillian always creating trouble, misery, changes, flights, dramas. No time to digest anything. And then she says I die when she leaves, that pain and war are good for me."

Djuna notices that although he is only forty years old, his hair is greying at the temple.

"Your eyes are full of wonder," he said, "as if you expected a miracle every day. I can't let you go now. I want to go places with you, obscure little places, just to be able to say: here I came with Djuna. I'm insatiable, you know. I'll ask you for the impossible. What it is, I don't know. You'll tell me, probably. You're quicker than I am. And you're the first woman with whom I feel I can be absolutely sincere. You make me happy because I can talk with you. I feel at ease with you. This is a little drunken, but you know what I mean. You always seem to know what I mean."

"You change from a wise old man to a savage. You're both timid and cruel too, aren't you?"

"There is something here it is impossible for Lillian to understand, or to break either. I feel we are friends. Don't you see? Friends. Christ, have a man and woman ever been friends, beyond love and beyond desire, and beyond everything, friends? Well, that is what I feel with you."

She hated the gayety with which she received these words, for that condemnation of her body to be the pale watcher, the understanding one upon whom others laid their burdens, laying their heads on her lap to sleep, to be lulled from others' wounds. And even as she hated her own goodness, she heard herself say quietly, out of the very core of this sense of justice: "The destroyers do not always destroy, Jay."

"You see more, you just see more, and what you see is there all right. You get at the core of everything."

And now she was caught between them, to be the witch of words, a silent swift shadow darkened by uncanny knowledge, forgetting herself, her human needs, in the unfolding of this choking blind relationship: Lillian and Jay lacerating each other because of their different needs.

Pale beauty of the watcher shining in the dark.

Both of them now, Jay and Lillian, entered Djuna's life by gusts, and left by gusts, as they lived.

She sat for hours afterwards sailing her lingering mind like a slow river boat down the feelings they had dispersed with prodigality.

"In my case," said Jay, alone with her, "what's difficult is to keep any image of myself clear. I have never thought about myself much. The first time I saw myself full length, as it were, was in you. I have grown used to considering your image of me as the correct one. Probably because it makes me feel good. I was like a wheel without a hub."

"And I'm the hub, now," said Djuna, laughing.

Jay was lying on the couch in the parlor, and she had left him to dress for an evening party. When she was dressed she opened the door and then stood before her long mirror perfuming herself.

The window was open on the garden and he said: "This is like a setting for Pelleas and Melisande. It is all a dream."

The perfume made a silky sound as she squirted it with the atomizer, touching her ear lobes, her neck. "Your dress is green like a princess," he said, "I could swear it is a green I have never seen before and will never see again. I could swear the garden is made of cardboard, that the trembling of the light behind you comes from the footlights, that the sounds are music. You are almost transparent there, like the mist of perfume you are throwing on yourself. Throw more perfume on yourself, like a fixative on a water color. Let me have the atomizer. Let me put perfume all over you so that you won't disappear and fade like a water color."

She moved towards him and sat on the edge of the couch: "You don't quite believe in me as a woman," she said, with an immense distress quite out of proportion to his fancy.

"This is a setting for Pelleas and Melisande," he said, "and I know that when you leave me for that dinner I will never see you again. Those incidents last at the most three hours, and the echoes of the music maybe a day. No more."

The color of the day, the color of Byzantine paintings, that gold which did not have the firm surface of lacquer, that gold made of a fine powder easily decomposed by time, a soft powdery gold which seemed on the verge of decomposing, as if each grain of dust, held together only by atoms, was ever ready to fall apart like a mist of perfume; that gold so thin in substance that it allowed one to divine the canvas behind it, the space in the painting, the presence of reality behind its thinness, the fibrous space lying behind the illusion, the absence of color and depth, the condition of emptiness and blackness underneath the gold powder. This gold powder which had fallen now on the garden, on each leaf of the trees, which was flowering inside the room, on her black hair, on the skin of his wrists, on his frayed suit sleeve, on the green carpet, on her green dress, on the bottle of perfume, on his voice, on her anxiety – the very breath of living, the very breath he and she took in to live and breathed out to live – that very breath could mow and blow it all down.

The essence, the human essence always evaporating where the dream installs itself.

The air of that summer day, when the wind itself had suspended its breathing, hung between the window and garden; the air itself could displace a leaf, could displace a word, and a displaced leaf or word might change the whole aspect of the day.

The essence, the human essence always evaporating where the dream installed itself and presided.

Every time he said he had been out the night before with friends and that he had met a woman, there was a suspense in Lillian's being, a moment of fear that he might add: I met the woman who will replace you. This moment was repeated for many years with the same suspense, the same sense of the fragility of love, without bringing any change in his love. A kind of superstition haunted her, running crosscurrent to the strength of the ties binding them, a sense of menace. At first because the love was all expansion and did not show its roots; and later, when the roots were apparent, because she expected a natural fading and death.

This fear appeared at the peak of their deepest moments, a precipice all around their ascensions. This fear appeared through the days of their tranquillity, as a sign of death rather than a sign of natural repose. It marked every moment of silence with the seal of a fatal secret. The greater the circle spanned by the attachment, the larger she saw the fissure through which human beings fall again into solitude.

The woman who personified this danger never appeared. His description gave no clues. Jay made swift portraits which he seemed to forget the next day. He was a man of many friends. His very ebullience created a warm passage but an onward flowing one, forming no grooves, fixing no image permanently. His enthusiasms were quickly burned out, sometimes in one evening. She never sought out these passing images.

Now and then he said with great simplicity: "You are the only one. You are the only one."

And then one day he said: "The other day I met a woman you would like. I was sorry you were not there. She is coming with friends this evening. Do you want to stay? You will see. She has the most extraordinary eyes."

"She has extraordinary eyes? I'll stay. I want to know her." (Perhaps if I run fast enough ahead of the present I will outdistance the shock. What is the difference between fear and intuition? How clearly I have seen what I imagine, as clearly as a vision. What is it I feel now, fear or premonition?)

Helen's knock on the door was vigorous, like an attack. She was very big and wore a severely tailored suit. She looked like a statue, but a statue with haunted eyes, inhuman eyes not made for weeping, full of animal glow. And the rest of her body a statue pinned down to its base, immobilized by a fear. She had the immobility of a Medusa waiting to transfix others into stone: hypnotic and cold, attracting others to her mineral glow.

She had two voices, one which fell deep like the voice of a man, and another light and innocent. Two women disputing inside of her.

She aroused a feeling in Lillian which was not human. She felt she was looking at a painting in which there was an infinity of violent blue. A white statue with lascivious Medusa hair. Not a woman but a legend with enormous space around her.

Her eyes were begging for an answer to an enigma. The pupils seemed to want to separate from the whites of the eyes.

Lillian felt no longer any jealousy, but a curiosity as in a dream. She did not feel any danger or fear in the meeting, only an enormous blue space in which a woman stood waiting. This space and grandeur around Helen drew Lillian to her.

Helen was describing a dream she often had of being carried away by a Centaur and Lillian could see the Centaur holding Helen's head, the head of a woman in a myth. People in myths were larger than human beings.

Helen's dreams took place in an enormous desert where she was lost among the prisons. She was tearing her hands to get free. The columns of these prisons were human beings all bound in bandages. Her own draperies were of sackcloth, the woolen robes of punishment.

And then came her questions to Lillian: "Why am I not free? I ran away from my husband and my two little girls, many years ago. I did not know it then, but I didn't want to be a mother, the mother of children. I wanted to be the mother of creations and dreams, the mother of artists, the muse and the mistress. In my marriage I was buried alive. My husband was a man without courage for life. We lived as if he were a cripple, and I a nurse. His presence killed the life in me so completely that I could hardly feel the birth of my children. I became afraid of nature, of being swallowed by the mountains, stifled by the forest, absorbed by the sea. I rebelled so violently against my married life that in one day I destroyed everything and ran away, abandoning my children, my home and my native country. But I never attained the life I had struggled to reach. My escape brought me no liberation. Every night I dream the same dream of prisons and struggles to escape. It is as if only my body escaped, and not my feelings. My feelings were left over there like roots dangling when you tear a plant too violently. Violence means nothing. And it does not free one. Part of my being remained with my children, imprisoned in the past. Now I have to liberate myself wholly, body and soul, and I don't know how. The violent gestures I make only tighten the knot of resistance around me. How can one liquidate the past? Guilt and regrets can't be shed like an old coat."

Then she saw that Lillian was affected by her story and she added: "I am grateful to Jay for having met you."

Only then Lillian remembered her painful secret. For a moment she wanted to lay her head on Helen's shoulder and confess to her:

"I only came because I was afraid of you. I came because I thought you were going to take Jay away from me." But now that Helen had revealed her innermost dreams and pains, Lillian felt: perhaps she needs me more than she needs Jay. For he cannot console. He can only make her laugh.

At the same time she thought that this was equally effective. And she remembered how much Jay liked audacity in women, how some feminine part of him liked to yield, liked to be chosen, courted. Deep down he was timid, and he liked audacity in women. Helen could be given the key to his being, if Lillian told her this. If Lillian advised her to take the first step, because he was a being perpetually waiting to be ignited, never set off by himself, always seeking in women the explosion which swept him along.

All around her there were signs, signs of danger and loss.

Without knowing consciously what she was doing, Lillian began to assume the role she feared Jay might assume. She became like a lover. She was full of attentiveness and thoughtfulness. She divined Helen's needs uncannily. She telephoned her at the moment Helen felt the deepest loneliness. She said the gallant words Helen wanted to hear. She gave Helen such faith as lovers give. She gave to the friendship an atmosphere of courtship which accomplished the same miracles as love. Helen began to feel enthusiasm and hunger again. She forgot her illness to take up painting, her singing, and writing. She recreated, redecorated the place she was living in. She displayed art in her dressing, care and fantasy. She ceased to feel alone.

On a magnificent day of sun and warmth Lillian said to her: "If I were a man, I would make love to you."

Whether she said this to help Helen bloom like a flower in

warmth and fervor, or to take the place of Jay and enact the courtship she had imagined, which she felt she had perhaps deprived Helen of, she did not know.

But Helen felt as rich as a woman with a new love.

At times when Lillian rang Helen's bell, she imagined Jay ringing it. And she tried to divine what Jay might feel at the sight of Helen's face. Every time she fully conceded that Helen was beautiful. She asked herself whether she was enhancing Helen's beauty with her own capacity for admiration. But then Jay too had this capacity for exalting all that he admired.

Lillian imagined him coming and looking at the paintings. He would like the blue walls. It was true he would not like her obsessions with disease, her fear of cancer. But then he would laugh at them, and his laughter might dispel her fears.

In Helen's bathroom, where she went to powder and comb her hair, she felt a greater anguish, because there she was nearer to the intimacy of Helen's life. Lillian looked at her kimono, her bedroom slippers, her creams and medicines as if trying to divine with what feelings Jay might look at them. She remembered how much he liked to go behind the scenes of people's lives. He liked to rummage among intimate belongings and dispel illusions. It was his passion. He would come out triumphantly with a jar: and this, what is this for? as if women were always seeking to delude him. He doubted the most simple things. He had often pulled at her eyelashes to make certain they were not artificial.

What would he feel in Helen's bathroom? Would he feel tenderness for her bedroom slippers? Why were there objects which inspired tenderness and others none. Helen's slippers did not inspire tenderness. Nothing about her inspired tenderness. But it might inspire desire, passion, anything else — even if she remained outside of one, like a sculpture, a painting, a form, not something which penetrated and enveloped one. But inhuman figures could inspire passion. Even if she were the statue in a Chirico painting, unable to mingle with human beings, even if she could not be impregnated by others or live inside of another all tangled in threads of blood and emotion.

When they went out together Lillian always expected the coincidence which would bring the three of them together to the same concert, the same exhibit, the same play. But if it never happened. They always missed each other. All winter long the coincidences of city life did not bring the three of them together. Lillian began to think that this meeting was not destined, that it was not she who was keeping them apart.

Helen's eyes grew greener and sank more and more into the myth. She could not feel. And Lillian felt as if she were keeping from her the man who might bring her back to life. Felt almost as if she were burying her alive by not giving her Jay.

Perhaps Lillian was imagining too much.

Meanwhile Helen's need of Lillian grew immense. She was not contented with Lillian's occasional visits. She wanted to fill the entire void of her life with Lillian. She wanted Lillian to stay over night when she was lonely. The burden grew heavier and heavier.

Lillian became frightened. In wanting to amuse and draw Helen away from her first interest in Jay, she had surpassed herself and become this interest.

Helen dramatized the smallest incident, suffered from insomnia, said her bedroom was haunted at night, sent for Lillian on every possible occasion.

Lillian was punished for playing the lover. Now she must be the husband, too. Helen had forgotten Jay but the exchange had left Lillian as a hostage.

Not knowing how to lighten the burden she said one day: "You ought to travel again. This city cannot be good for you. A place where you have been lonely and unhappy for so long must be the wrong place."

That very night there was a fire in Helen's house, in the apartment next to hers. She interpreted this as a sign that Lillian's intuitions for her were wise. She decided to travel again.

They parted at the corner of a street, gayly, as if for a short separation. Gayly, with green eyes flashing at one another. They lost each other's address. It all dissolved very quickly, like a dream.

And then Lillian felt free again. Once again she had worn the warrior armòr to protect a core of love. Once again she had worn the man's costume.

Jay had not made her woman, but the husband and mother of his weakness.

⁘

Lillian confessed to Jay that she was pregnant. He said: "We must find the money for an abortion." He looked irritated. She waited. She thought he might slowly evince interest in the possibility of a child. He revealed only an increased irritation. It disturbed his plans, his enjoyment. The mere idea of a child was an intrusion. He let her go alone to the doctor. He expressed resentment. And then she understood.

She sat alone one day in their darkened room.

She talked to the child inside of her.

"My little one not born yet, I feel your small feet kicking against my womb. My little one not born yet, it is very dark in the room you and I are sitting in, just as dark as it must be for you inside of me, but it must be sweeter for you to be lying in the warmth than it is for me to be seeking in this dark room the joy of not knowing, not feeling, not seeing; the joy of lying still in utter warmth and this darkness. All of us forever seeking this warmth and this darkness, this being alive without pain, this being alive without anxiety, fear or loneliness. You are impatient to live, you kick with your small feet, but you ought to die. You ought to die in warmth and darkness, you ought to die because you are a child without a father. You will not find on earth this father as large as the sky, big enough to hold your whole being and your fears, larger than house or church. You will not find a father who will lull you and cover you with his greatness and his warmth. It would be better if you died inside of me, quietly, in the warmth and in the darkness."

Did the child hear her? At six months she had a miscarriage and lost it.

∴

Lillian was giving a concert in a private home which was like a temple of treasures. Paintings and people had been collected with expert and exquisite taste. There was a concentration of beautiful women so that one was reminded of a hothouse exhibit.

The floor was so highly polished there were two Lillians, two white pianos, two audiences.

The piano under her strong hands became small like a child's piano. She overwhelmed it, she tormented it, crushed it. She played with all her intensity, as if the piano must be possessed or possess her.

The women in the audience shivered before this *corps a corps.*

Lillian was pushing her vigor into the piano. Her face was full of vehemence and possessiveness. She turned her face upwards as if to direct the music upwards, but the music would not rise, volatilize itself. It was too heavily charged with passion.

She was not playing to throw music into the blue space, but to reach some climax, some impossible union with the piano, to reach that which men and women could reach together. A moment of pleasure, a moment of fusion. The passion and the blood in her rushed against the ivory notes and overloaded them. She pounded the coffer of the piano as she wanted her own body pounded and shattered. And the pain on her face was that of one who reached neither sainthood nor pleasure. No music rose and passed out of the window, but a sensual cry, heavy with unspent forces. . . .

Lillian storming against her piano, using the music to tell all how she wanted to be stormed with equal strength and fervor.

This tidal power was still in her when the women moved towards her to tell her it was wonderful. She rose from the piano as if she would engulf them, the smaller women; she embraced them with all the fervor of unspent intensity that had not reached a climax — which the music, like too delicate a vessel, the piano with too delicate a frame, had not been able to contain.

It was while Lillian was struggling to tear from the piano what the piano could not possibly give her that Djuna's attention was wafted towards the window.

In the golden salon, with the crystal lamps, the tapestries and the paintings, there were immense bay windows, and Djuna's chair had been placed in one of the recesses, so that she sat on the borderline between the perfumed crowd and the silent, static garden.

It was late in the afternoon, the music had fallen back upon the people like a heavy storm cloud which could not be dispersed to lighten and lift them, the air was growing heavy, when her eyes caught the garden as if in a secret exposure. As everyone was looking at Lillian, Djuna's sudden glance seemed to have caught the garden unaware, in a dissolution of peace and greens. A light rain had washed the faces of the leaves, the knots in the tree trunks stared with aged eyes, the grass was drinking, there was a sensual humidity as if leaves, trees, grass and wind were all in a state of caress.

The garden had an air of nudity.

Djuna let her eyes melt into the garden. The garden had an air of nudity, of efflorescence, of abundance, of plenitude.

The salon was gilded, the people were costumed for false roles, the lights and the faces were attenuated, the gestures were starched – all but Lillian whose nature had not been stylized, compressed or gilded, and whose nature was warring with a piano.

Music did not open doors.

Nature flowered, caressed, spilled, relaxed, slept.

In the gilded frames, the ancestors were mummified forever, and descendants took the same poses. The women were candied in perfume, conserved in cosmetics, the men preserved in their elegance. All the violence of naked truths had evaporated, volatilized within gold frames.

And then, as Djuna's eyes followed the path carpeted with

detached leaves, her eyes encountered for the first time three full-length mirrors placed among the bushes and flowers as casually as in a boudoir. Three mirrors.

The eyes of the people inside could not bear the nudity of the garden, its exposure. The eyes of the people had needed the mirrors, delighted in the fragility of reflections. All the truth of the garden, the moisture, and the worms, the insects and the roots, the running sap and the rotting bark, had all to be reflected in the mirrors.

Lillian was playing among vast mirrors. Lillian's violence was attenuated by her reflection in the mirrors.

The garden in the mirror was polished with the mist of perfection. Art and artifice had breathed upon the garden and the garden had breathed upon the mirror, and all the danger of truth and revelation had been exorcised.

Under the house and under the garden there were subterranean passages and if no one heard the premonitory rumblings before the explosion, it would all erupt in the form of war and revolution.

The humiliated, the defeated, the oppressed, the enslaved. Woman's misused and twisted strength. . . .

BREAD AND THE WAFER

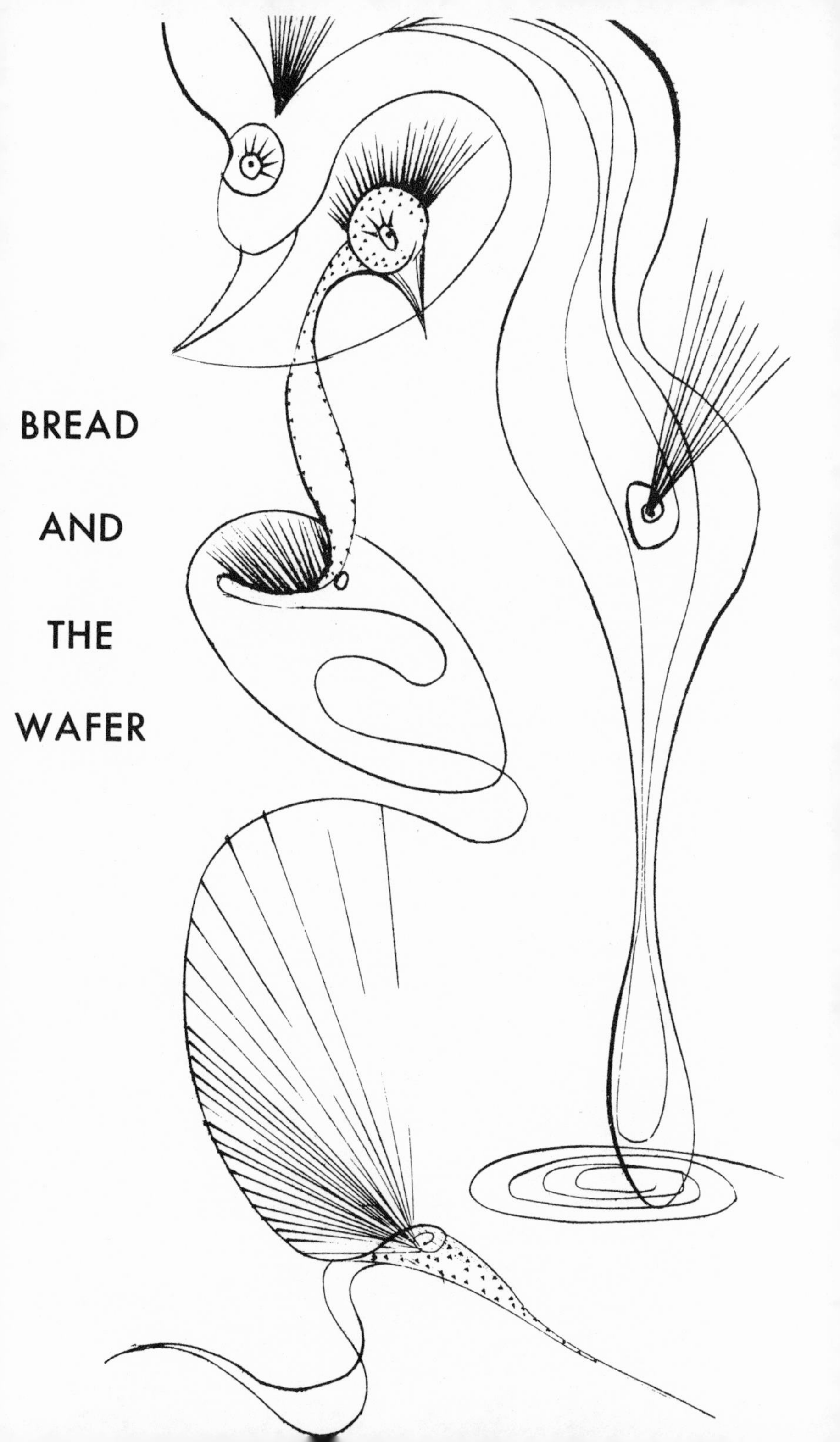

WHEN Jay was not talking or painting he sang. He sang under his breath or loudly according to his occupation. He dressed and ate to a rhythm, as if he were executing a primitive ritual with his big body that had not been quite chiselled off with the finish of a classical sculptor but whose outline had remained rugged as if it were not yet entirely separated from the wood or stone out of which it had been carved. One expected to feel the roughness of it as when one touched a clay figure before it had been thrust into the potter's oven.

He had retained so much of the animal, a graceful awkwardness in his walk, strong rhythmic gestures in full accord with the pull of the muscles, an animal love of stretching, yawning, relaxing, of sleeping anywhere, of obeying every impulse of his body. A body without nerves or tensions.

When he stood upon his well-planted, well-separated feet it was as if like a tree he would immediately take root there. As he had taken roots lustily in Paris now, in the cafés, in his studio, in his life with Lillian.

Wherever he found himself he was well, as if the living roots of his body could sprout in any ground, at any time, under any sky. His preference went, however, to artificial lights, crowds, and he grew, talked, and laughed best in the center of a stream of people.

If he were waiting he would fill the waiting with explosions of song, or fall into enthusiastic observations. The spectacle of the street was enough for him; whatever was there was enough for him, for his boundless satisfaction.

Placed before a simple meal he would begin his prestidigitations: this steak is wonderful . . . how *good* it is. How awfully good! And the onions. . . . He made sounds of delight. He poured his enthusiasm over the meal like a new condiment. The steak began to glow, to expand, to multiply under the warmth of his fervor. Every dish was wrapped in amorous appreciation, as if it had been brought to the table with a fire burning under it and was flaming in rum like a Christmas pudding.

"Good, good, good," said his palate, said his roseate cheeks, said his bowed assenting head, said his voice, all expanding in prodigious additions, as if he were pushing multiple buttons of delight, and colors burst from the vegetables, meat, salad, cheese and wine. Even the parsley assumed a festive air like a birthday candle on a cake. "Ah, ah, ah, the salad!" he said, pouring over it a voice like an unguent along with the olive oil.

His pleasure donned the white cap of the proud chef playing gay scales of flavors, festooning the bread and wine with the high taste of banquets.

The talk, too, burst its boundaries. He started a discussion, let it take fire and spread, but the moment it took too rigid a form he began to laugh, spraying it, liquefying it in a current of gaiety.

To laugh. To laugh. "I'm not laughing at you. I'm not laughing at anyone, at anybody. I just can't help myself. I don't care a bit, not a bit, who's right."

"But you must care," said Faustin, speaking through a rigid mask of sadness which made his face completely static, and one was surprised that the words could come through the closed mouth. "You must care, you must hold on to something."

"I never hold on," said Jay. "Why hold on? Whatever you hold on to dies. There comes Colette. Sit here, Colette. How was the trade today? Colette, these people are talking about holding on. You must hold on, you must care, they say. Do you hold on, Colette? They pass like a stream, don't they, and you'd be surprised if the same ones bobbed up continuously, surprised and maybe bored. It's a good stream, isn't it, just a stream that does not nestle into you to become an ulcer, a good washing stream that cleanses as it flows, and flows clean through."

With this he drank fully from his Pernod, drank indeed as if the stream of absinthe, of ideas, feelings, talk, should pass and change every day guided only by thirst.

"You're drunk," said Colette. "You don't make sense."

"Only the drunks and the insane make sense, Colette, that's where you're wrong. Only the drunks and the insane have discarded the unessential for chaos, and only in chaos there is richness."

"If you go on this way," said Faustin, his finger pointing upward like a teacher of Sanskrit, "someone will have to take care of you while you spill in all directions recklessly. You'll need taking care of, for yours is no real freedom but an illusion of freedom, or perhaps just rebellion. Chaos always turns out to be the greatest trap of all in which you'll find yourself more securely imprisoned than anyone."

At the words "taking care" Jay had turned automatically towards Lillian and read in her eyes that fixed, immutable love which was his compass.

When Faustin was there at the café conversation would always start at the top of a pyramid without any gradual ascension. It would start with the problems of form, being and becoming, physiognomics, destiny versus incident, the coming of the fungoid era, the middle brain and the tertiary moon!

Faustin talked to build. He insisted that each talk should be a complete brick to add to a careful construction. He always started to draw on the marble-top table or on the tablecloth: this is our first premise, this is our second premise, and now we will reach the third. No sooner had he made on the table the semblance of a construction than there would come into Jay's eyes an absinthe glint which was not really the drink but some layer of his being which the drink had peeled away, which was hard, cruel, mischievous. His phrases would begin to break and scatter, to run wild like a machine without springs, gushing forth from the contradictory core of him which refused all crystallizations.

It happened every time the talk approached a definite conclusion, every time some meaning was about to be extracted from confusion. It was as if he felt that any attempt at understanding were a threat to the flow of life, to his enjoyment. As if understanding would threaten the tumultuous current or arrest it.

They were eating in a small café opposite the Gare St. Lazare, a restaurant wide open on the street. They were eating on the street and it was as if the street were full of people who were eating and drinking with them.

With each mouthful Lillian swallowed, she devoured the noises of the street, the voices and the echoes they dropped, the swift glances which fell on her like pieces of lighted wick from guttering candles. She was only the finger of a whole bigger body, a body hungry, thirsty, avid.

The wine running down her throat was passing through the throat of the world. The warmth of the day was like a man's hand on her breast, the smell of the street like a man's breath on her neck. Wide open to the street like a field washed by a river.

Shouts and laughter exploded near them from the art students on their way to the *Quatz' Arts* Ball. Egyptians and Africans in feather and jewelry, with the sweat shining on their brown painted bodies. They ran to catch the bus and it was like a heaving sea of glistening flesh shining between colored feathers and barbaric jewelry, with the muscles swelling when they laughed.

A few of them entered the restaurant, shouting and laughing. They circled around their table, like savages dancing around a stake.

The street organ was unwinding *Carmen* from its roll of tinfoil voices.

⁘

The same restaurant, another summer evening; but Jay is not there. The wine has ceased passing down Lillian's throat. It has no taste. The food does not seem rich. The street is separated from the restaurant by little green bushes she had not noticed before; the noises seem far from her, and the faces remote. Everything now happens outside, and not within her own body. Everything is distant and separate. It does not flow inside of her and carry her away.

Because Jay is nor there? Does it mean it was not she who had drunk the wine, eaten the food, but that she had eaten and drunk through the pores of his pleasure and his appetite? Did she receive her pleasure, her appetite, through his gusto, his lust, his throat?

That night she had a dream: Jay had become her iron lung. She was lying inside of him and breathing through him. She felt a great anxiety, and thought: if he leaves me then I will die. When Jay laughed she laughed; when he enjoyed she enjoyed. But all the time there was this fear that if he left her she would no longer eat, laugh or breathe.

When he welcomed friends, was at ease in groups, accepted and included all of life, she experienced this openness, this total absence of retraction through him. When alone, she still carried some constriction which interfered with deep intakes of life and people. She had thought that by yielding to him they would be removed.

She felt at times that she had fallen in love with Jay's freedom, that she had dreamed he would set her free, but that somehow or other he had been unable to accomplish this.

At night she had the feeling that she was being possessed by a cannibal.

His appetite. The gifts she made him of her feelings. How he devoured the response of her flesh, her thoughts about him, her awareness of him. As he devoured new places, new people, new impressions. His gigantic devouring spirit in quest of substance.

Her fullness constantly absorbed by him, all the changes in her, her dissolutions and rebirths, all this could be thrown into the current of his life, his work, and be absorbed like twigs by a river.

He had the appetite of the age of giants.

He could read the fattest books, tackle the most immense paintings, cover the vastest territories in his wanderings, attack the most solemn system of ideas, produce the greatest quantity of work. He excluded nothing: everything was food. He could eat the trival and the puerile, the ephemeral and the gross, the scratchings on a wall, the phrase of a passerby, the defect on a face, the pale sonata streaming from a window, the snoring of a beggar on a bench, flowers on the wallpaper of a hotel room, the odor of cabbage on a stairway, the haunches of a bareback rider in the circus. His eyes devoured details, his hands leaped to grasp.

His whole body was like a sensitive sponge, drinking, eating, absorbing with a million cells of curiosity.

She felt caught in the immense jaws of his desire, felt herself dissolving, ripping open to his descent. She felt herself yielding up to his dark hunger, her feelings smouldering, rising from her like smoke from a black mass.

Take me, take me, take my gifts and my moods and my body and my cries and my joys and my submissions and my yielding and my terror and my abandon, take all you want.

He ate her as if she were something he wanted to possess inside of his body like a fuel. He ate her as if she were a food he needed for daily sustenance.

She threw everything into the jaws of his desire and hunger. Threw all she had known, experienced and given before. She gathered all to feed his ravenousness; she went into the past and brought back her past selves, she took the present self and the future self and threw them into the jaws of his curiosity, flung them before the greed of his questions.

The red lights from a hotel sign shone into the studio. A red well. A charging, a hoofing, a clanging, a rushing through the body. Thumping. The torrent pressure of a machine, panting, sliding back and forth, back and forth.

Swing. Swing. The bed-like stillness and downiness of summer foliage. Roll. Roll. Clutch and fold. Steam. Steam. The machine on giant oiled gongs yielding honey, rivers of honey on a bed of summer foliage. The boat slicing open the lake waters, ripples extending to the tips of the hair and the roots of the toes.

No stronger sea than this sea of feelings she swam into with him, was rolled by, no waves like the waves of desire, no foam like the foam of pleasure. No sand warmer than skin, the sand and quicksands of caresses. No sun more powerful than the sun of desire, no snow like the snow of her resistance melting in blue joys, no earth anywhere as rich as flesh.

She slept, she fell into trances, she was lost, she was renewed, she was blessed, pierced by joy, lulled, burned, consumed, purified, born and reborn within the whale belly of the night.

⁘

At the beginning of their life together he had constantly reverted to his childhood as if to deposit in her hands all the mementoes of his early voyages.

In all love's beginnings this journey backwards takes place: the desire of every lover to give his loved one all of his different selves, from the beginning.

What was most vivid in Jay's memory was the treachery of his parents.

"I was about six years old when a brand-new battleship docked at the Brooklyn Navy yard. All the boys in the neighborhood had been taken to see it but me. They kept describing it in every detail until I could dream of it as if I had seen it myself. I wanted desperately for my father to take me to it. He kept postponing the visit. Then one day he told me to wash my hands and ears carefully, to put on my best suit and said he was taking me to see the battleship. I washed myself as never before. I walked beside my father neat, and proud and drunk with gaiety. I kept telling him the number of guns we would see, the number of portholes. My father listened with apparent interest. He walked me into a doctor's office instead, where I had my tonsils taken out. The pain was a million times multiplied by the shock of disillusion, of betrayal, by the violent contrast between my dream, my expectations, and the brutal reality of the operation."

As he told this story it was clear to Lillian that he still felt the shock of the deception and had never forgiven his father. The intensity of the wish had been made even greater by the poverty of his childhood which made the visit to the battleship a unique pleasure discussed by his playmates for a whole year and not easily forgotten.

"One very cold, snowy night my mother and I were walking towards the river. I was very small, five years old maybe. My mother was walking too fast for me, and I felt terribly cold, especially my hands. My mother carried a muff. Every now and then she took her right hand out of the muff to grab mine when we crossed the streets. The warmth of her hand warmed me all through. Then she would drop my hand again and nestle hers back in her muff. I began to weep: I wanted to put my hand inside of her muff but she wouldn't let me. I wept and raged as if it were a matter of life and death – probably was, for me. I wanted the warmth and her naked hands. The more I wept and pulled at the muff the harsher my mother got. Finally she slapped my hand so I would let the muff go."

As he told this his blue eyes became the eyes of an irrevocably angry child. Lillian could see clear through his open eyes as through the wrong end of a telescope, a diminutive Jay raging, cold and thwarted, with his blue frozen hands reaching for his mother's muff.

This image was not being transmitted to Lillian the woman, but to the responsive child in herself understanding and sharing his anger and disillusion. It was the child in herself who received it as it sank through and beyond the outer layer of the woman who sat there listening with a woman's full body, a woman's face. But of this response there was no outer sign showing for Jay to see: the child in her lay so deeply locked within her, so deeply buried, that no sign of its existence or of its response was apparent. It did not beckon through her eyes which showed only a woman's compassion, nor alter her gestures nor the pose of her body which was the pose of a woman listening to a child and looking at his smallness without herself changing stature. At this moment, like Jay, she could have slipped out of her maturity, of her woman's body, and exposed her child's face, eyes, movements, and then Jay would have seen it, known that he had communicated with it, touched it by way of his own childhood, and the child might have met the child and become aware of its similar needs.

By her attitude she did not become one with him in this return to his past self. What she overtly extended to him was one who seemed done with her child self and who would replace the harsh mother, extend the muff and the warm naked hands.

She became, at that instant, indelibly fixed in his eyes not as another child with possibly equal needs, but as the stronger one in possession of the power to dispense to all *his* needs.

From now on was established an inequality in power: he was the cold and hungry one, she the muff and the warm naked hands.

From now on her needs, concealed and buried as mere interferences with the accomplishment of this role, were condemned to permanent muteness. Strong direction was given to her activity as the muff, as the provider of innumerable battleships in compensation for the one he had been cheated of. Giving to him on all levels, from book to blanket to phonograph to fountain pen to food, was always and forever the battleship he had dreamed and not seen. It was the paying off of a debt to the cheated child.

Lillian did not know then that the one who believes he can pay this early debt meets a bottomless well. Because the first denial has set off a fatality of revenge which no amount of giving can placate. Present in every child and criminal is this conviction that no retribution will repair the injury done. The man who was once starved may revenge himself upon the world not by stealing just once, or by stealing only what he needs, but by taking from the world an endless toll in payment of something irreplaceable, which is the lost faith.

This diminutive Jay who appeared in the darkness when he evoked his childhood was also a personage who could come nearer to her own frightened self without hurting her than the assertive, rather ruthless Jay who appeared in the daytime when he resumed his man's life. When he described his smallness and how he could enter saloons to call for his father without having to swing the doors open, it seemed to Lillian that she could encompass this small figure better in the range of her vision than the reckless, amorphous, protean Jay whose personality flowed into so many channels like swift mercury.

When Jay described the vehemence, the wildness, the hunger with which he went out into the streets to play, it seemed to her that he was simultaneously describing and explaining the vehemence, the hunger, the wildness with which he went out at night now and left her alone, so that the present became strangely innocent in her mind.

When he talked about his impulses towards other women he took on the expression not of a man who had enjoyed another woman sensually, but of a gay, irrepressible child whose acts were absolutely uncontrollable; it became no longer infidelity but a childish, desperate eagerness to "go to the street and play."

She saw him in the present as the same child needing to boast of his conquests out of a feeling of helplessness, needing to be admired, to win many friends, and thus she attenuated in herself the anxiety she experienced at his many far-flung departures from her.

When she rebelled at times he looked completely baffled by her rebellions, as if there were nothing in his acts which could harm her. She always ended by feeling guilty: he had given her his entire self to love, including the child, and now, out of noblesse oblige, she could not possibly act . . . like his harsh mother!

He looked at the sulphur-colored Pernod and drank it.

He was in the mood to paint his self-portrait for anyone who wanted to listen: this always happened after someone had attacked his painting, or claimed some overdue debt.

So Jay drank Pernod and explained: I'm like Buddha who chose to live in poverty. I abandoned my first wife and child for a religious life. I now depend on the bowl of rice given to me by my followers.

"What do you teach?" asked a young man who was not susceptible to the contagión of Jay's gayety.

"A life from which all suffering is absent."

But to the onlooker who saw them together, Lillian, ever alert to deflect the blows which might strike at him, it seemed much more as if Jay had merely unburdened all sadnesses upon her rather than as if he had found a secret for eliminating them altogether. His disciples inevitably discovered they, too, must find themselves a Lillian to achieve his way of life.

"I'm no teacher," said Jay, "I'm just a happy man. I can't explain how I arrived at such a state." He pounded his chest with delight. "Give me a bowl of rice and I will make you as joyous as I am."

This always brought an invitation to dinner.

"Nothing to worry about," he always said to Lillian. "Someone will always invite me to dinner."

In return for the dinner Jay took them on a guided tour of his way of life. Whoever did not catch his mood could go overboard. He was no initiator. Let others learn by osmosis!

But this was only one of his self-portraits. There were other days when he did not like to present himself as a laughing man who communicated irresponsibility and guiltlessness, but as the great barbarian. In this mood he exulted the warriors, the invaders, the pillagers, the rapers. He believed in violence. He saw himself as Attila avenging the impurities of the world by bloodshed. He saw his paintings then as a kind of bomb.

As he talked he became irritated with the young man who had asked him what he taught, for Jay noticed that he walked back and forth constantly but not the whole length of the studio. He would take five long steps, stop mechanically, and turn back like an automaton. The nervous compulsion disturbed Jay and he stopped him: "I wish you'd sit down."

"Excuse me, I'm really sorry," he said, stopping dead. A look of anxiety came to his face. "You see, I've just come out of jail. In jail I could only walk five steps, no more. Now when I'm in a large room, it disturbs me. I want to explore it, familiarize myself with it, at the same time I feel compelled to walk no further."

"You make me think of a friend I had," said Jay, "who was very poor and a damned good painter and of the way he escaped from his narrow life. He was living at the Impasse Rouet, and as you know probably, that's the last step before you land at the Hospital, the Insane Asylum or the Cemetery. He lived in one of those houses set far back into a courtyard, full of studios as bare as cells. There was no heat in the house and most of the windows were cracked and let the wind blow through. Those who owned stoves, for the most part, didn't own any coal. Peter's studio had an additional anomaly: it had no windows, only a transom. The door opened directly on the courtyard. He had no stove, a cot whose springs showed through the gored mattress. No sheets, and only one old blanket. No doorbell, of course. No electricity, as he couldn't pay the bill. He used candles, and when he had no money for candles he got fat from the butcher and burnt it. The concierge was like an old octopus, reaching everywhere at once with her man's voice and inquisitive whiskers. Peter was threatened with eviction when he hit upon an idea. Every year, as you know, foreign governments issued prizes for the best painting, the best sculpture. Peter got one of the descriptive pamphlets from the Dutch Embassy where he had a friend. He brought it to the concierge and read it to her, then explained: fact one: he was the only Dutch painter in Paris.

Fact two: a prize would be given to the best painting produced by a Dutchman, amounting to half a million francs. The concierge was smart enough to see the point. She agreed to let the rent slide for a month, to lend him money for paints and a little extra change for cigarettes while he painted something as big as the wall of his cell. In return, with the prize money, he promised to buy her a little house in the country for her old age – with garden. Now he could paint all day. It was spring; he left his door open and the concierge settled in the courtyard with her heavy red hands at rest on her lap and thought that each brush stroke added to her house and garden. After two months she got impatient. He was still painting, but he was also eating, smoking cigarettes, drinking aperitifs and even sleeping at times more than eight hours. Peter rushed to the Embassy and asked his friend to pay him an official call. The friend managed to borrow the official car with the Dutch coat of arms and paid the painter a respectful visit. This reassured her for another month. Every evening they read the booklet together: 'the prize will be handed over in cash one week after the jury decides upon its value. . . .' The concierge's beatitude was contagious. The entire house benefited from her mellowness. Until one morning when the newspapers published the name and photograph of the genuine Dutch painter who had actually won the prize and then without warning she turned into a cyclone. Peter's door was locked. She climbed on a chair to look through the transom to make sure he was not asleep or drunk. To her great horror she saw a body hanging from the ceiling. He had hung himself! She called for help. The police forced the door open. What they cut down was a mannequin of wax and old rags, carefully painted by Peter.

"The funny thing," added Jay after a pause, "is that after this his luck turned. When he hung his effigy he seemed to have killed the self who had been a failure."

The visitors left.

Then all the laughter in him subsided into a pool of serenity. His voice became soft. Just as he loved the falsities of his roles he loved also to rest from these pranks and attitudes and crystallize in the white heat of Lillian's faith.

And when all the gestures and talk seemed lulled, suddenly he sprang up again with a new mood, a fanatic philosopher who walked up and down the studio punctuating the torrent of his ideas with fist blows on the tables. A nervous lithe walk, while he churned ideas like leaves on a pyre which never turned to ash.

Then all the words, the ideas, the memories, were drawn together like the cords of a hundred kites and he said:

"I'd like to work now."

Lillian watched the transformation in him. She watched the half open mouth close musingly, the scattered talk crystallizing. This man so easily swayed, caught, moved, now collecting his strength again. At that moment she saw the big man in him, the man who appeared to be merely enjoying recklessly, idling, roaming, but deep down set upon a terribly earnest goal: to hand back to life all the wealth of material he had collected, intent on making restitution to the world for what he had absorbed with his enormous creator's appetite.

There remained in the air only the echoes of his resonant voice, the hot breath of his words, the vibration of his pounding gestures.

She rose to lock the door of the studio upon the world. She drew in long invisible bolts. She pulled in rustless shutters. Silence. She imprisoned within herself that mood and texture of Jay which would never go into his work, or be given or exposed to the world, that which she alone could see and know.

⁘

While Lillian slept Jay reassembled his dispersed selves.

At this moment the flow in him became purposeful.

In his very manner of pressing the paint tube there was intensity; often it spurted like a geyser, was wasted, stained his clothes and the floor. The paint, having appeared in a minor explosion, proceeded to cause a major one on the canvas.

The explosion caused not a whole world to appear, but a shattered world of fragments. Bodies, objects, cities, trees, animals were all splintered, pierced, impaled.

It was actually a spectacle of carnage.

The bodies were dismembered and every part of them misplaced. In the vast dislocation eyes were placed where they had never visited a body, the hands and feet were substituted for the face, the faces bore four simultaneous facets with one empty void between. Gravity was lost, all relation between the figures were like those of acrobats. Flesh became rubber, trees flesh, bones became plumage, and all the life of the interior, cells, nerves, sinew lay exposed as by a merely curious surgeon not concerned with closing the incisions. All his painter's thrusts opening, exposing, dismembering in the violent colors of reality.

The vitality with which he exploded, painted dissolution and disintegration, with which his energy broke familiar objects into unfamiliar components, was such that people who walked into a room full of his painting were struck only with the power and force of these brilliant fragments as by an act of birth. That they were struck only by broken pieces of an exploded world, they did not see. The force of the explosion, the weight, density and brilliance was compelling.

To each lost, straying piece of body or animal was often added the growth and excrescences of illness, choking moss on southern trees, cocoons of the unborn, barnacles and parasites.

It was Jay's own particular jungle in which the blind warfare of insects and animals was carried on by human beings. The violence of the conflicts distorted the human body. Fear became muscular twistings like the tangled roots of trees, dualities sundered them in two separate pieces seeking separate lives. The entire drama took place at times in stagnant marshes, in petrified forests where every human being was a threat to the other.

The substance that could weld them together again was absent. Through the bodies irretrievable holes had been drilled and in place of a heart there was a rubber pump or a watch.

The mild, smiling Jay who stepped out of these infernos always experienced a slight tremor of uneasiness when he passed from the world of his painting to Lillian's room. If she was awake she would want to see what he had been doing. And she was always inevitably shocked. To see the image of her inner nightmares exposed affected her as the sight of a mirror affects a cat or a child. There was always a moment of strained silence.

This underground of hostility she carried in her being, of which her body felt only the blind impacts, the shocks, was now clearly projected.

Jay was always surprised at her recoil, for he could see how Lillian was a prolongation of this warfare on canvas, how at the point where he left violence and became a simple, anonymous, mild-mannered man, it was she who took up the thread and enacted the violence directly upon people.

But Lillian had never seen herself doing it.

Jay would say: "I wish you wouldn't quarrel with everyone, Lillian."

"I wish you wouldn't paint such horrors. Why did you paint Faustin without a head? That's what he's proudest of – his head."

"Because that's what he should lose, to come alive. You hate him too. Why did you hand him his coat the other night in such a way that he was forced to leave?"

In the daylight they repudiated e[illegible] other. At night their bodies recognized a familiar substance: gunpowder, and they made their peace together.

In the morning it was he who went out for bread, butter and milk for breakfast, while she made the coffee.

When she locked the studio for the night, she locked out anxiety. But when Jay got into his slack morning working clothes and stepped out jauntily, whistling, he had a habit of locking the door again – and in between, anxiety slipped in again.

He locks the door, he has forgotten that I am here.

Thus she interpreted it, because of her feeling that once he had taken her, he deserted her each time anew. No contact was ever continuous with him. So he locked the door, forgot she was there, deserted her.

When she confessed this to Djuna, Djuna who had continued to write for Lillian the Chinese dictionary of counter-interpretations, she laughed: "Lillian, have you ever thought that he might be locking you in to keep you for himself?"

⁘

Lillian was accurate in her feeling that when Jay left the studio he was disassociated from her, and not from her alone, but from himself.

He walked out in the street and become one with the street. His mood became the mood of the street. He dissolved and became eye, ear, smile.

There are days when the city exposes only its cripples, days when the bus must stop close to the curb to permit a one-legged man to board it, days when a man without legs rests his torso on a rolling stand and propels himself with his hands, days when a head is held up by a pink metal truss, days when blind men ask to be guided, and Jay knew as he looked, absorbing every detail, that he would paint them, even though had he been consulted all the cripples of the world would be destroyed excepting the smiling old men who sat on benches beatifically drunk, because they were his father. He had so many fathers, for he was one to see the many. *I believe we have a hundred fathers and mothers and lovers all interchangeable, and that's the flaw in Lillian, for her there is only one mother, one father, one husband, one lover, one son, one daughter, irreplaceable, unique – her world is too small. The young girl who just passed me with lightning in her eyes is my daughter. I could take her home as my daughter in place of the one I lost. The world is full of fathers, whenever I need one I only need to stop and talk to one . . . this one sitting there with a white beard and a captain's cap . . .*

"Do you want a cigarette, Captain?"

"I'm no captain, Monsieur, I was a Legionnaire, as you can see by my beard. Are you sure you haven't a butt or two? I'd rather have a butt. I like my independence, you know, I collect butts. A cigarette is charity. I'm a hobo, you know, not a beggar."

His legs were wrapped in newspapers. "Because of the varicose veins. They sort of bother me in the winter. I could stay with the nuns there, they would take care of me. But imagine having to get up every morning at six at the sound of a bell, of having to eat exactly at noon, and then at seven and having to sleep at nine. I'm better here. I like my independence." He was filling his pipe with butts.

Jay sat beside him.

"The nuns are not bad to me. I collect crusts of old bread from the garbage cans and I sell them to the Hospital for the soup they serve to pregnant women."

"Why did you leave the Legion?"

"During my campaigns I received letters from an unknown godmother. You can't imagine what those letters were, Monsieur, I haven't got them because I wore them out reading them there, in the deserts. They were so warm I could have heated my hands over them if I had been fighting in a cold country. Those letters made me so happy that on my first furlough I looked her up. That was quite a task, believe me, she had no address! She sold bananas from a little cart, and she slept under the bridges. I spent my furlough sitting with her like this with a bottle of red wine. It was a good life; I deserted the Legion."

He again refused a cigarette and Jay walked on.

The name of a street upon an iron plate, Rue Dolent, Rue Dolent decomposed for him into dolorous, doliente, douleur. The plate is nailed to the prison wall, the wall of China, of our chaos and our mysteries, the wall of Jericho, of our religions and our guilts, the wall of lamentation, the wall of the prison of Paris. Wall of soot, encrusted dust. No prison breaker ever crumbled this wall, the darkest and longest of all leaning heavily upon the little Rue Dolent Doliente Douleur which, although on the free side of the wall, is the saddest street of all Paris. On one side are men whose crimes were accomplished in a moment of rage, rebellion, violence. On the other, grey figures too afraid to hate, to rebel, to kill openly. On the free side of the wall they walk with iron bars in their hearts and stones on their feet carrying the balls and chains of their obsessions. Prisoners of their weakness, of their self-inflicted illnesses and slaveries. No need of guards and keys! They will never escape from themselves, and they only kill others with the invisible death rays of their impotence.

He did not know any longer where he was walking. The personages of the street and the personages of his paintings extended into each other, issued from one to fall into the other, fell into the work, or out of it, stood now with, now without, frames. The man on the sliding board, had he not seen him before in Coney Island when he was a very young man and walking with a woman he loved? This half-man had followed them persistently along the boardwalk, on a summer night made for caresses, until the woman had recoiled from his pursuit and left both the half-man and Jay. Again the man on wheels had appeared in his dream, but this time it was his mother in a black dress with black jet beads on it as he had seen her once about to attend a funeral. Why he should deprive his mother of the lower half of her body, he didn't know. No fear of incest had ever barred his way to women, and he had always been able to want them all, and the more they looked like his mother the better.

He saw the seven hard benches of the pawnshop where he had spent so many hours of his life in Paris waiting to borrow a little cash on his paintings, and felt the bitterness he had tasted when they underestimated his work! The man behind the counter had eyes dilated from appraising objects. Jay laughed out loud at the memory of the man who had pawned his books and continued to read them avidly until the last minute like one condemned to future starvation. He had painted them all pawning their arms and legs, after seeing them pawn the stove that would keep them warm, the coat that would save them from pneumonia, the dress that would attract customers. A grotesque world, hissed the Dean of Critics. A distorted world. *Well and good. Let them sit for three hours on one of the seven benches of the Paris pawnshop. Let them walk through the Rue Dolent. Perhaps I should not be allowed to go free, perhaps I should be jailed with the criminals. I feel in sympathy with them. My murders are committed with paint. Every act of murder might awaken people to the state of things that produced it, but soon they fall asleep again, and when the artist awakens them they are quick to take revenge. Very good that they refuse me money and honors, for thus they keep me in these streets and exposing what they do not wish me to expose. My jungle is not the innocent one of Rousseau. In my jungle everyone meets his enemy. In the underworld of nature debts must be paid in the same specie: no false money accepted. Hunger with hunger, pain with pain, destruction with destruction.*

The artist is there to keep accounts.

⁘

From his explorations of the Dome, the Select, the Rotonde, Jay once brought back Sabina, though with these two people it would be difficult to say which one guided the other home or along the street, since both of them had this aspect of overflowing rivers rushing headlong to cover the city, making houses, cafés, streets and people seem small and fragile, easily swept along. The uprooting power of Jay's impulses added to Sabina's mobility reversed the whole order of the city.

Sabina brought in her wake the sound and imagery of fire engines as they tore through the streets of New York alarming the heart with the violent gong of catastrophe.

All dressed in red and silver, the tearing red and silver siren cutting a pathway through the flesh. The first time one looked at Sabina one felt: everything will burn!

Out of the red and silver and the long cry of alarm, to the poet who survives in a human being as the child survives in him, to this poet Sabina threw an unexpected ladder in the middle of the city and ordained: climb!

As she appeared, the orderly alignment of the city gave way before this ladder one was invited to climb, standing straight in space like the ladder of Baron Munchausen which led to the sky.

Only Sabina's ladder led to fire.

As she walked heavily towards Lillian from the darkness of

the hallway into the light of the door Lillian saw for the first time the woman she had always wanted to know. She saw Sabina's eyes burning, heard her voice so rusty and immediately felt drowned in her beauty. She wanted to say: I recognize you. I have often imagined a woman like you.

Sabina could not sit still. She talked profusely and continuously with feverish breathlessness, like one in fear of silence. She sat as if she could not bear to sit for long, and when she walked she was eager to sit down again. Impatient, alert, watchful, as if in dread of being attacked; restless and keen, making jerking gestures with her hands, drinking hurriedly, speaking rapidly, smiling swiftly and listening to only half of what was said to her.

Exactly as in a fever dream, there was in her no premeditation, no continuity, no connection. It was all chaos – her erratic gestures, her unfinished sentences, her sulky silences, her sudden walks through the room, her apologizing for futile reasons (I'm sorry, I lost my gloves), her apparent desire to be elsewhere.

She carried herself like one totally unfettered who was rushing and plunging on some fiery course. She could not stop to reflect.

She unrolled the film of her life stories swiftly, like the accelerated scenes of a broken machine, her adventures, her escapes from drug addicts, her encounters with the police, parties at which indistinct incidents took place, hazy scenes of flagellations in which no one could tell whether she had been the flagellator or the victim, or whether or not it had happened at all.

A broken dream, with spaces, reversals, contradictions, galloping fantasies and sudden retractions. She would say: "he lifted my skirt," or "we had to take care of the wounds," or "the policeman was waiting for me and I had to swallow the drug to save my friends," and then as if she had written this on a blackboard she took a huge sponge and effaced it all by a phrase which was meant to convey that perhaps this story had happened to someone else, or she may have read it, or heard it at a bar, and as soon as this was erased she began another story of a beautiful girl who was employed in a night club and whom Sabina had insulted, but if Jay asked why she shifted the scene, she at once effaced it, cancelled it, to tell about something else she had heard and not seen at the night club at which she worked.

The faces and the figures of her personages appeared only half drawn, and when one just began to perceive them another face and figure were interposed, as in a dream, and when one thought one was looking at a woman it was a man, an old man, and when one approached the old man who used to take care of her, it turned out to be the girl she lived with who looked like a younger man she had first loved and this one was metamorphosed into a whole group of people who had cruelly humiliated her one evening. Somewhere in the middle of the scene Sabina appeared as the woman with gold hair, and then later as a woman with black hair, and it was equally impossible to keep a consistent image of whom she had loved, betrayed, escaped from, lived with, married, lied to, forgotten, deserted.

She was impelled by a great confessional fever which forced her to lift a corner of the veil, but became frightened if anyone listened or peered at the exposed scene, and then she took a giant sponge and rubbed it all out, to begin somewhere else, thinking that in confusion there was protection. So Sabina beckoned and lured one into her world, and then blurred the passageways, confused the images and ran away in fear of detection.

From the very first Jay hated her, hated her as Don Juan hated Dona Juana, as the free man hates the free woman, as man hates in woman this freedom in passion which he grants solely to himself. Hated her because he knew instinctively that she regarded him as he regarded woman: as a possible or impossible lover.

He was not for her a man endowed with particular gifts, standing apart from other men, irreplaceable as Lillian saw him, unique as his friends saw him. Sabina's glance measured him as he measured women: endowed or not endowed as lovers.

She knew as he did, that none of the decorations or dignities conferred upon a man or woman could alter the basic talent or lack of talent as a lover. No title of architect emeritus will confer upon them the magic knowledge of the body's structure. No prestidigitation with words will replace the knowledge of the secret places of responsiveness. No medals for courage will confer the graceful audacities, the conquering abductions, the exact knowledge of the battle of love, when the moment for seduction, when for consolidation, when for capitulation.

The trade, art and craft that cannot be learned, which requires a divination of the finger tips, the accurate reading of signals from the fluttering of an eyelid, an eye like a microscope to catch the approval of an eyelash, a seismograph to catch the vibrations of the little blue nerves under the skin, the capacity to prognosticate from the direction of the down as from the inclination of the leaves some can predict rain, tell where storms are brooding, where floods are threatening, tell which regions to leave alone, which to invade, which to lull and which to take by force.

No decorations, no diplomas for the lover, no school and no traveller's experience will help a man who does not hear the beat, tempo and rhythms of the body, catch the ballet leaps of desire at their highest peak, perform the acrobatics of tenderness and lust, and know all the endless virtuosities of silence.

Sabina was studying his potentialities with such insolence, weighing the accuracy of his glance. For there is a black lover's glance well known to women versed in this lore, which can strike at the very center of woman's body, which plants its claim as in a perfect target.

Jay saw in her immediately the woman without fidelity, capable of all desecrations. That a woman should do this, wear no wedding ring, love according to her caprice and not be in bondage to the one. (A week before he was angry with Lillian for considering him as the unique and irreplaceable one, because it conferred on him a responsibility he did not wish to assume, and he was wishing she might consider an understudy who would occasionally relieve him of his duties!)

For one sparkling moment Jay and Sabina faced each other in the center of the studio, noting each other's defiance, absorbing this great mistrustfulness which instantly assails the man and women who recognize in each other the law-breaking lovers; erecting on this basic mutual mistrust the future violent attempts to establish certitude.

Sabina's dress at first like fire now appeared, in the more tangible light of Lillian's presence, as made of black satin, the texture most similar to skin. Then Lillian noticed a hole in Sabina's sleeve, and suddenly she felt ashamed not to have a hole in her sleeve too, for somehow, Sabina's poverty, Sabina's worn sandals, seemed like the most courageous defiance of all, the choice of a being who had no need of flawless sleeves or new sandals to feel complete.

Lillian's glance which usually remained fixed upon Jay, grazing lightly over others, for the first time absorbed another human being as intently.

Jay looked uneasily at them. This fixed attention of Lillian revolving around him had demanded of him, the mutable one, something he could not return, thus making him feel like a man accumulating a vast debt in terms he could never meet.

In Sabina's fluctuating fervors he met a challenge: she gave him a feeling of equality. She was well able to take care of herself and to answer treachery with treachery.

Lillian waited at the corner of the Rue Auber. She would see Sabina in full daylight advancing out of a crowd. She would make certain that such an image could materialize, that Sabina was not a mirage which would melt in the daylight.

She was secretly afraid that she might stand there at the corner of the Rue Auber exactly as she had stood in other places watching the crowd, knowing no figure would come out of it which would resemble the figures in her dreams. Waiting for Sabina she experienced the most painful expectancy: she could not believe Sabina would arrive by these streets, cross such a boulevard, emerge from a mass of faceless people. What a profound joy to see her striding forward, wearing her shabby sandals and her shabby black dress with royal indifference.

"I hate daylight," said Sabina, and her eyes darkened with anger. The dark blue rings under her eyes were so deep they marked her flesh. It was as if the flesh around her eyes had been burned away by the white heat and fever of her glance.

They found the place she wanted, a place below the level of the street.

Her talk like a turbulent river, like a broken necklace spilled around Lillian.

"It's a good thing I'm going away. You would soon unmask me."

At this Lillian looked at Sabina and her eyes said so clearly: "I want to become blind with you," that Sabina was moved and turned her face away, ashamed of her doubts.

"There are so many things I would love to do with you, Lillian. With you I would take drugs. I would not be afraid."

"You afraid?" said Lillian, incredulously. But one word rose persistently to the surface of her being, one word which was like a rhythm more than a word, which beat its tempo as soon as Sabina appeared. Each step she took with Sabina was marked as by a drum beat with the word: danger danger danger danger.

"I have a feeling that I want to be you, Sabina. I never wanted to be anyone but myself before."

"How can you live with Jay, Lillian? I hate Jay. I feel he is like a spy. He enters your life only to turn around afterwards and caricature. He exposes only the ugly."

"Only when something hurts him. It's when he gets hurt that he destroys. Has he caricatured you?"

"He painted me as a whore. And you know that isn't me. He has such an interest in evil that I told him stories. . . . I hate him."

"I thought you loved him," said Lillian simply.

All Sabina's being sought to escape Lillian's directness in a panic. Behind the mask a thousand smiles appeared, behind the eyelids ageless deceptions.

This was the moment. If only Sabina could bring herself to say what she felt: Lillian, do not trust me. I want Jay. Do not love me, Lillian, for I am like him. I take what I want no matter who is hurt.

"You want to unmask me, Lillian."

"If I were to unmask you, Sabina, I would only be revealing myself: you act as I would act if I had the courage. I see you exactly as you are, and I love you. You should not fear exposure, not from me."

This was the moment to turn away from Jay who was bringing her not love, but another false role of play, to turn towards Lillian with the truth, that a real love might take place.

Sabina's face appeared to Lillian as that of a child drowning behind a window. She saw Sabina as a child struggling with her terror of the truth, considering before answering what might come closest to the best image of herself she might give Lillian. Sabina would not say the truth but whatever conformed to what she imagined Lillian expected of her, which was in reality not at all what Lillian wanted of her, but what she, Sabina, thought necessary to her idealized image of herself. What Sabina was feverishly creating always was the reverse of what she acted out: a woman of loyalty and faithfulness. To maintain this image at all costs she ceased responding to Lillian's soft appeal to the child in need of a rest from pretenses.

"I don't deny Jay is a caricaturist, but only out of revengefulness. What have you done to deserve his revenge?"

Again Sabina turned her face away.

"I know you're not a *femme fatale*, Sabina. But didn't you want him to think you were?"

With this peculiar flair she had for listening to the buried child in human beings, Lillian could hear the child within Sabina whining, tired of its inventions grown too cumbersome, weary of its adornments, of its disguises. Too many costumes, valances, gold, brocade, veils, to cover Sabina's direct thrusts towards what she wanted, and meanwhile it was this audacity, this directness, this unfaltering knowledge of her wants which Lillian loved in her, wanted to learn from her.

But a smile of immeasurable distress appeared in Sabina, and then was instantly effaced by another smile: the smile of seduction. When Lillian was about to seize upon the distress, to enter the tender, vulnerable regions of her being, then Sabina concealed herself again behind the smile of a woman of seduction.

Pity, protection, solace, they all fell away from Lillian like gifts of trivial import, because with the smile of seduction Sabina assumed simultaneously the smile of an all-powerful enchantress.

Lillian forgot the face of the child in distress, hungrily demanding a truthful love, and yet, in terror that this very truth might destroy the love. The child face faded before this potent smile to which Lillian succumbed.

She no longer sought the meaning of Sabina's words. She looked at Sabina's blonde hair tumbling down, at her eyebrows peaked upward, at her smile slanting perfidiously, a gem-like smile which made a whirlpool of her feelings.

A man passed by and laughed at their absorption.

"Don't mind, don't mind," said Sabina, as if she were familiar with this situation. "I won't do you any harm."

"You can't do me any harm."

Sabina smiled. "I destroy people without meaning to. Everywhere I go things become confused and terrifying. For you I would like to begin all over again, to go to New York and become a great actress, to become beautiful again. I won't appear any more with clothes that are held together with safety pins! I've been living stupidly, blindly, doing nothing but drinking, smoking, talking. I'm afraid of disillusioning you, Lillian."

They walked down the streets aimlessly, unconscious of their surroundings, arm in arm with a joy that was rising every moment, and with every word they uttered. A swelling joy that mounted with each step they took together and with the occasional brushing of their hips as they walked.

The traffic eddied around them but everything else, houses and trees were lost in a fog. Only their voices distinct, carrying such phrases as they could utter out of their female labyrinth of oblique perceptions.

Sabina said: "I wanted to telephone you last night. I wanted to tell you how sorry I was to have talked so much. I knew all the time I couldn't say what I wanted to say."

"You too have fears, although you seem so strong," said Lillian.

"I do everything wrong. It's good that you don't ever ask questions about facts. Facts don't matter. It's the essence that matters. You never ask the kind of question I hate: what city? what man? what year? what time? Facts. I despise them."

Bodies close, arm in arm, hands locked together over her breast. She had taken Lillian's hand and held it over her breast as if to warm it.

The city had fallen away. They were walking into a world of their own for which neither could find a name.

They entered a softly lighted place, mauve and diffuse, which enveloped them in velvet closeness.

Sabina took off her silver bracelet and put it around Lillian's wrist.

"It's like having your warm hand around my wrist. It's still warm, like your own hand. I'm your prisoner, Sabina."

Lillian looked at Sabina's face, the fevered profile taut, so taut that she shivered a little, knowing that when Sabina's face turned towards her she could no longer see the details of it for its blazing quality. Sabina's mouth always a little open, pouring forth that eddying voice which gave one vertigo.

Lillian caught an expression on her face of such knowingness that she was startled. Sabina's whole body seemed suddenly charged with experience, as if discolored from it, filled with violet shadows, bowed down by weary eyelids. In one instant she looked marked by long fevers, by an unconquerable fatigue. Lillian could see all the charred traces of the fires she had traversed. She expected her eyes and hair to turn ashen.

But the next moment her eyes and hair gleamed more brilliantly than ever, her face became uncannily clear, completely innocent, an innocence which radiated like a gem. She could shed her whole life in one moment of forgetfulness, stand absolutely washed of it, as if she were standing at the very beginning of it.

So many questions rushed to Lillian's mind, but now she knew Sabina hated questions. Sabina's essence slipped out between the facts. So Lillian smiled and was silent, listening merely to Sabina's voice, the way its hoarseness changed from rustiness to a whisper, a faint gasp, so that the hotness of her breath touched her face.

She watched her smoke hungrily, as if smoking, talking and moving were all desperately necessary to her, like breathing, and she did them all with such reckless intensity.

When Lillian and Sabina met one night under the red light of the café they recognized in each other similar moods: they would laugh at him, the man.

"He's working so hard, so hard he's in a daze," said Lillian. "He talks about nothing but painting."

She was lonely, deep down, to think that Jay had been at his work for two weeks without noticing either of them. And her loneliness drew her close to Sabina.

"He was glad we were going out together, he said it would give him a chance to work. He hasn't any idea of time – he doesn't even know what day of the week it is. He doesn't give a damn about anybody or anything."

A feeling of immense loneliness invaded them both.

They walked as if they wanted to walk away from their mood, as if they wanted to walk into another world. They walked up the hill of Montmartre with little houses lying on the hillside like heather. They heard music, music so off tune that they did not recognize it as music they heard every day. They slid into a shaft of light from where this music came – into a room which seemed built of granified smoke and crystallized human breath. A room with a painted star on the ceiling, and a wooden, pock-marked Christ nailed to the wall. Gusts of weary, petrified songs, so dusty with use. Faces like empty glasses. The musicians made of rubber like the elastic, rubber-soled night.

We hate Jay tonight. We hate man.

The craving for caresses. Wanting and fighting the want. Both frightened by the vagueness of their desire, the indefiniteness of their craving.

A rosary of question marks in their eyes.

Sabina whispered: "Let's take drugs tonight."

She pressed her strong knee against Lillian, she inundated her with the brilliance of her eyes, the paleness of her face.

Lillian shook her head, but she drank, she drank. No drink equal to the state of war and hatred. No drink like bitterness.

Lillian looked at Sabina's fortuneteller's eyes, and at the taut profile.

"It takes all the pain away; it wipes out reality."

She leaned over the table until their breaths mingled.

"You don't know what a relief it is. The smoke of opium like fog. It brings marvelous dreams and gayety. Such gayety, Lillian. And you feel so powerful, so powerful and content. You don't feel any more frustration, you feel that you are lording it over the whole world with marvellous strength. No one can hurt you then, humiliate you, confuse you. You feel you're soaring over the world. Everything becomes soft, large, easy. Such joys, Lillian, as you have never imagined. The touch of a hand is enough . . . the touch of a hand is like going the whole way. . . . And time . . . how time flies. The days pass like an hour. No more straining, just dreaming and floating. Take drugs with me, Lillian."

Lillian consented with her eyes. Then she saw that Sabina was looking at the Arab merchant who stood by the door with his red Fez, his kimono, his slippers, his arms loaded with Arabian rugs and pearl necklaces. Under the rugs protruded a wooden leg with which he was beating time to the jazz.

Sabina laughed, shaking her whole body with drunken laughter. "You don't know, Lillian . . . this man . . . with his wooden leg . . . you never can tell . . . he may have some. There was a man once, with a wooden leg like that. He was arrested and they found that his wooden leg was packed with snow. I'll go and ask him."

And she got up with her heavy, animal walk, and talked to the rug merchant, looking up at him alluringly, begging, smiling up at him in the same secret way she had of smiling at Lillian. A burning pain invaded Lillian to see Sabina begging. But the merchant shook his head, smiled innocently, shook his head firmly, smiled again, offering his rugs and the necklaces.

When she saw Sabina returning empty handed, Lillian drank again, and it was like drinking fog, long draughts of fog.

They danced together, the floor turning under them like a phonograph record. Sabina dark and potent, leading Lillian.

A gust of jeers seemed to blow through the place. A gust of jeers. But they danced, cheeks touching, their cheeks chalice white. They danced and the jeers cut into the haze of their dizziness like a whip. The eyes of the men were insulting them. The eyes of men called them by the name the world had for them. Eyes. Green, jealous. Eyes of the world. Eyes sick with hatred and contempt. Caressing eyes, participating. Eyes ransacking their conscience. Stricken yellow eyes of envy caught in the flare of a match. Heavy torpid eyes without courage, without dreams. Mockery, frozen mockery from the frozen glass eyes of the loveless.

Lillian and Sabina wanted to strike those eyes, break them, break the bars of green wounded eyes, condemning them. They wanted to break the walls confining them, suffocating them. They wanted to break out from the prison of their own fears, break every obstacle. But all they found to break were glasses. They took their glasses and broke them over their shoulders and made no wish, but looked at the fragments of the glasses on the floor wonderingly as if their mood of rebellion might be lying there also, in broken pieces.

Now they danced mockingly, defiantly, as if they were sliding beyond the reach of man's hands, running like sand between their insults. They scoffed at those eyes which brimmed with knowledge for they knew the ecstasy of mystery and fog, fire and orange fumes of a world they had seen through a slit in the dream. Spinning and reeling and falling, spinning and turning and rolling down the brume and smoke of a world seen through a slit in the dream.

The waiter put his ham-colored hand on Sabina's bare arm: "You've got to get out of here, you two!"

⁘

They were alone.

They were alone without daylight, without past, without any thought of the resemblance between their togetherness and the union of other women. The whole world was being pushed to one side by their faith in their own uniqueness. All comparisons proudly discarded.

Sabina and Lillian alone, innocent of knowledge, and innocent of other experiences. They remembered nothing before this hour: they were innocent of associations. They forgot what they had read in books, what they had seen in cafés, the laughter of men and the mocking participation of other women. Their individuality washed down and effaced the world: they stood at the beginning of everything, naked and innocent of the past.

They stood before the night which belonged to them as two women emerging out of sleep. They stood on the first steps of their timidity, of their faith, before the long night which belonged to them. Blameless of original sin, of literary sins, of the sin of premeditation.

Two women. Strangeness. All the webs of ideas blown away. New bodies, new souls, new minds, new words. They would create it all out of themselves, fashion their own reality. Innocence. No roots dangling into other days, other nights, other men or women. The potency of a new stare into the face of their desire and their fears.

Sabina's sudden timidity and Lillian's sudden awkwardness. Their fears. A great terror slashing through the room, cutting icily through them like a fallen sword. A new voice. Sabina's breathless and seeking to be lighter so as to touch the lightness of Lillian's voice like a breath now, an exhalation, almost a voicelessness because they were so frightened.

Sabina sat heavily on the edge of the bed, her earthy weight like roots sinking into the earth. Under the weight of her stare Lillian trembled.

Their bracelets tinkled.

The bracelets had given the signal. A signal like the first tinkle of beads on a savage neck when they enter a dance. They took their bracelets off and put them on the table, side by side.

The light. Why was the light so still, like the suspense of their blood? Still with fear. Like their eyes. Shadeless eyes that dared neither open, nor close, nor melt.

The dresses. Sabina's dress rolled around her like long sea weed. She wanted to turn and drop it on the floor but her hands lifted it like a Bayadere lifting her skirt to dance and she lifted it over her head.

Sabina's eyes were like a forest; the darkness of a forest, a watchfulness behind ambushes. Fear. Lillian journeyed into the darkness of them, carrying her blue eyes into the red-brown ones. She walked from the place where her dress had fallen holding her breasts as if she expected to be mortally thrust.

Sabina loosened her hair and said: "You're so extraordinarily white." With a strange sadness, like a weight, she spoke, as if it were not the white substance of Lillian but the whiteness of her newness to life which Sabina seemed to sigh for. "You're so white, so white and smooth." And there were deep shadows in her eyes, shadows of one old with living: shadows in the neck, in her arms, on her knees, violet shadows.

Lillian wanted to reach out to her, into these violet shadows. She saw that Sabina wanted to be she as much as she wanted to be Sabina. They both wanted to exchange bodies, exchange faces. There was in both of them the dark strain of wanting to become the other, to deny what they were, to transcend their actual selves. Sabina desiring Lillian's newness, and Lillian desiring Sabina's deeply marked body.

Lillian drank the violet shadows, drank the imprint of others, the accumulation of other hours, other rooms, other odors, other caresses. How all the other loves clung to Sabina's body, even though her face denied this and her eyes repeated: I have forgotten all. How they made her heavy with the loss of herself, lost in the maze of her gifts. How the lies, the loves, the dreams, the obscenities, the fevers weighed down her body, and how Lillian wanted to become leadened with her, poisoned with her.

Sabina looked at the whiteness of Lillian's body as into a mirror and saw herself as a girl, standing at the beginning of her life unblurred, unmarked. She wanted to return to this early self. And Lillian wanted to enter the labyrinth of knowledge, to the very bottom of the violet wells.

Through the acrid forest of her being there was a vulnerable opening. Lillian trod into it lightly. Caresses of down, moth invasions, myrrh between the breasts, incense in their mouths. Tendrils of hair raising their heads to the wind in the finger tips, kisses curling within the conch-shell necks. Tendrils of hair bristling and between their closed lips a sigh.

"How soft you are, how soft you are," said Sabina.

They separated and saw it was not this they wanted, sought, dreamed. Not this the possession they imagined. No bodies touching would answer this mysterious craving in them to become each other. Not to possess each other but to become each other. Not to take, but to imbibe, absorb, change themselves. Sabina carried a part of Lillian's being, Lillian a part of Sabina, but they could not be exchanged through an embrace. It was not that.

Their bodies touched and then fell away, as if both of them had touched a mirror, their own image upon a mirror. They had felt the cold wall, they had felt the mirror that never appeared when they were taken by man. Sabina had merely touched her own youth, and Lillian her free passions.

As they lay there the dawn entered the room, a grey dawn which showed the dirt on the window panes, the crack in the table, the stains on the walls. Lillian and Sabina sat up as if the dawn had opened their eyes. Slowly they descended from dangerous heights, with the appearance of daylight and the weight of their fatigue.

With the dawn it was as if Jay had entered the room and were now lying between them. Every cell of their dream seemed to burst at once, with the doubt which had entered Lillian's mind.

If she had wanted so much to be Sabina so that Jay might love in her what he admired in Sabina, could it be that Sabina wanted of Lillian this that made Jay love her?

"I feel Jay in you," she said.

The taste of sacrilege came to both their mouths. The mouths he kissed. The women whose flavor he knew. The one man within two women. Jealousy, dormant all night; now lying at their side, between their caresses, slipping in between them like an enemy.

(Lillian, Lillian, if you arouse hatred between us, you break a magic alliance! He is not as aware of us as we are of each other. We have loved in each other all he has failed to love and see. Must we awake to the great destructiveness of rivalry, of war, when this night contained all that slipped between his fingers!)

But jealousy had stirred in Lillian's flesh. Doubt was hardening and crystallizing in Lillian, crystallizing her features, her eyes, tightening her mouth, stiffening her body. She shivered with cold, with the icy incision of this new day which was laying everything bare.

Bare eyes looking at each other with naked, knife-pointed questions.

To stare at each other they had to disentangle their hair, Sabina's long hair having curled around Lillian's neck.

Lillian left the bed. She took the bracelets and flung them out of the window.

"I know, I know," she said violently, "you wanted to blind me. If you won't confess, he will. It's Jay you love, not me. Get up. I don't want him to find us here together. And he thought we loved each other!"

"I do love you, Lillian."

"Don't you dare say it," shouted Lillian violently, all her being now craving wildly for complete devastation.

They both began to tremble.

Lillian was like a foaming sea, churning up wreckage, the debris of all her doubts and fears.

⁘

Their room was in darkness. Then came Jay's laughter, creamy and mould-breaking. In spite of the darkness Lillian could feel all the cells of his body alive in the night, vibrating with abundance. Every cell with a million eyes seeing in the dark.

"A fine dark night in which an artist might well be born," he said. "He must be born at night, you know, so that no one will notice that his parents gave him only seven months of human substance. No artist has the patience to remain nine months in the womb. He must run away from home. He is born with a mania to complete himself, to create himself. He is so multiple and amorphous that his central self is constantly falling apart and is only recomposed by his work. With his imagination he can flow into all the moulds, multiply and divide himself, and yet whatever he does, he will always be two."

"And require two wives?" asked Lillian.

"I need you terribly," he said.

Would the body of Sabina triumph over her greater love?

"There are many Sabinas in the world, but only one like you," said Jay.

How could he lie so close and know only what she chose to tell him, knowing nothing of her, of her secret terrors and fear of loss.

He was only for the joyous days, the days of courage, when she could share with him all the good things he brought with his passion for novelty and change.

But he knew nothing of her; he was no companion to her sadness. He could never imagine anyone else's mood, only his own. His own were so immense and loud, they filled his world and deafened him to all others. He was not concerned to know whether she could live or breathe within the dark caverns of his whale-like being, within the whale belly of his ego.

Somehow he had convinced her that this expansiveness was a sign of bigness. A big man could not belong to one person. He had merely overflowed into Sabina, out of over-richness. And they would quarrel some day. Already he was saying: "I suspect that when Sabina gives one so many lies it is because she has nothing else to give but mystery, but fiction. Perhaps behind her mysteries there is nothing."

But how blinded he was by false mysteries! Because Sabina made such complicated tangles of everything – mixing personalities, identities, missing engagements, being always elsewhere than where she was expected to be, chaotic in her hours, elusive about her occupations, implying mystery and suspense even when she said goodbye . . . calling at dawn when everyone was asleep, and asleep when everyone else was awake. Jay with his indefatigable curiosity was easily engaged in unravelling the tangle, as if every tangle had a meaning, a mystery.

But Lillian knew, too, how quickly he could turn about and

ridicule if he were cheated, as he often was, by his blind enthusiasms. How revengeful he became when the mysteries were false.

"If only Sabina would die," thought Lillian, "if she would only die. She does not love him as I do."

Anxiety oppressed her. Would he push everything into movement again, disperse her anxieties with his gayety, carry her along in his reckless course?

Lillian's secret he did not detect: that of her fear. Once her secret had almost pierced through, once when Jay had stayed out all night. From her room she could see the large lights of the Boulevard Montparnasse blinking maliciously, Montparnasse which he loved and those lights, and the places where he so easily abandoned himself as he gave himself to everything that glittered,— rococo women, spluttering men in bars, anyone who smiled, beckoned, had a story to tell.

She had waited with the feeling that where her heart had been there was now a large hole; no heart or blood beating anymore but a drafty hole made by a precise and rather large bullet.

Merely because Jay was walking up and down Montparnasse in one of his high drunken moods which had nothing to do with drink but with his insatiable thirst for new people, new smiles, new words, new stories.

Each time the white lights blinked she saw his merry smile in his full mouth, each time the red lights blinked she saw his cold blue eyes detached and mocking, annihilating the mouth in a daze of blue, iced gayety. The eyes always cold, the mouth warm, the eyes mocking and the mouth always repairing the damage done. His eyes that would never turn inward and look into the regions of deep events, the regions of personal explorations: his eyes intent on not seeing discords or dissolutions, not seeing the missing words, the lost treasures, the wasted hours, the shreds of the dispersed self, the blind mobilities.

Not to see the dark night of the self his eyes rose frenziedly to the surface seeking in fast-moving panoramas merely the semblance of riches. . . .

"Instead of love there is appetite," thought Lillian. "He does not say: 'I love you,' but 'I need you.' Our life is crowded like a railroad station, like a circus. He does not feel things where I feel them: the heart is definitely absent. That's why mine is dying, it has ceased to pound tonight, it is being slowly killed by his hardness."

Away from him she could always say: he does not feel. But as soon as he appeared she was baffled. His presence carried such a physical glow that it passed for warmth. His voice was warm like the voice of feeling. His gestures were warm, his hands liked touch. He laid his hands often on human beings, and one might think it was love. But it was just a physical warmth, like the summer. It gave off heat like a chemical, but no more.

"He will die of hardness, and I from feeling too much. Even when people knock on the door I have a feeling they are not knocking on wood but on my heart. All the blows fall directly on my heart."

Even pleasure had its little stabs upon the heart. The perpetual heart-murmur of the sensibilities.

"I wish I could learn his secret. I would love to be able to go out for a whole night without feeling all the threads that bind me to him, feeling my love for him all around me like a chastity belt."

And now he was lying still on the breast of her immutable love and she had no immutable love upon which to lay her head, no one to return to at dawn.

He sat up lightly saying: "Oh, Sabina has no roots!"

"And I'm strangling in my roots," thought Lillian.

He had turned on the light to read now, and she saw his coat hugging the back of the chair, revealing in the shape of its shoulders the roguish spirit that had played in it. If she could only take the joys he gave her, his soft swagger, the rough touch of his coat, the effervescence of his voice when he said: that's good. Even his coat seemed to be stirring with his easy flowing life, even to his clothes he gave the imprint of his liveliness.

To stem his outflowing would be like stemming a river of life. She would not be the one to do it. When a man had decided within himself to live out every whim, every fancy, every impulse, it was a flood for which no Noah's Ark had ever been provided.

⁘

Lillian and Djuna were walking together over dead autumn leaves that crackled like paper. Lillian was weeping and Djuna was weeping with her and for her.

They were walking through the city as it sank into twilight and it was as if they were both going blind together with the bitterness of their tears. Through this blurred city they walked hazily and half lost, the light of a street lamp striking them now and then like a spotlight throwing into relief Lillian's distorted mouth and the broken line of her neck where her head fell forward heavily.

The buses came upon them out of the dark, violently, with a deafening clatter, and they had to leap out of their way, only to continue stumbling through dark streets, crossing bridges, passing under heavy arcades, their feet unsteady on the uneven cobblestones as if they had both lost their sense of gravity.

Lillian's voice was plaintive and monotonous, like a lamentation. Her blue eyes wavered but always fixed on the ground as if the whole structure of her life lay there and she were watching its consummation.

Djuna was looking straight before her, through and beyond the dark, the lights, the traffic, beyond all the buildings. Eyes fixed, immobile like glass eyes, as if the curtain of tears had opened a new realm.

Lillian's phrases surged and heaved like a turgid sea. Unformed, unfinished, dense, heavy with repetitions, with recapitulations, with a baffled, confused bitterness and anger.

Djuna found nothing to answer, because Lillian was talking about God, the God she had sought in Jay.

"Because he had the genius," she said, "I wanted to serve him, I wanted to make him great. But he is treacherous, Djuna, I am more confused and lost now than before I knew him. It isn't only his betrayals with women, Djuna, it's that he sees no one as they are. He only adds to everyone's confusions. I put myself wholly in his hands. I wanted to serve someone who would create something wonderful, and I also thought he would help me to create myself. But he is destructive, and he is destroying me."

This seeking of man the guide in a dark city, this aimless wandering through the streets touching men and seeking the guide – this was a fear all women had known . . . seeking the guide in men, not in the past, or in mythology, but a guide with a living breath who might create one, help one to be born as a woman, a guide they wished to possess for themselves alone, in their own isolated woman's soul. The guide for woman was still inextricably woven with man and with man's creation.

Lillian had thought that Jay would create her because he was the artist, that he would be able to see her as clearly as she had seen in him the great painter, but Jay's inconsistencies bewildered her. She had placed her own image in his hands for him to fashion: make of me a big woman, someone of value.

His own chaos had made this impossible.

"Lillian, no one should be entrusted with one's image to fashion, with one's self-creation. Women are moving from one circle to another, rising towards independence and self-creation. What you're really suffering from is from the pain of parting with your faith, with your old love when you wish to renew this faith and preserve the passion. You're being thrust out of one circle into another and it is this which causes you so much fear. You know you cannot lean on Jay, but you don't know what awaits you, and you don't trust your own awareness."

Lillian thought that she was weeping because Jay had said: "Leave me alone, or let me work, or let me sleep."

"Oh, Lillian, it's such a struggle to emerge from the past clean of regrets and memories and of the desire to regress. No one can accept failure."

She wanted to take Lillian's hand and make her raise her head and lead her into a new circle, raise her above the pain and confusion, above the darkness of the present.

These sudden shafts of light upon them could not illumine

where the circle of pain closed and ended and woman was raised into another circle. She could not help Lillian emerge out of the immediacy of her pain, leap beyond the strangle-hold of the present.

And so they continued to walk unsteadily over what Lillian saw merely as the dead leaves of his indifference.

⁘

Jay and Lillian lived in the top floor studio of a house on the Rue Montsouris, on the edge of Montparnasse – a small street without issue lined with white cubistic villas.

When they gave a party the entire house opened its doors from the ground floor to the roof, since all the artists knew each other. The party would branch off into all the little street with its quiet gardens watched by flowered balconies.

The guests could also walk down the street to the Park Montsouris lake, climb on a boat and fancy themselves attending a Venetian feast.

First came the Chess Player, as lean, brown, polished, and wooden in his gestures as a chess piece; his features sharply carved and his mind set upon a perpetual game.

For him the floors of the rooms were large squares in which the problem was to move the people about by the right word. To control the temptation to point such a person to another he kept his hands in his pockets and used merely his eyes. If he were talking to someone his eyes would design a path in the air which his listener could not help but follow. His glance having caught the person he had selected made the invisible alliance in space and

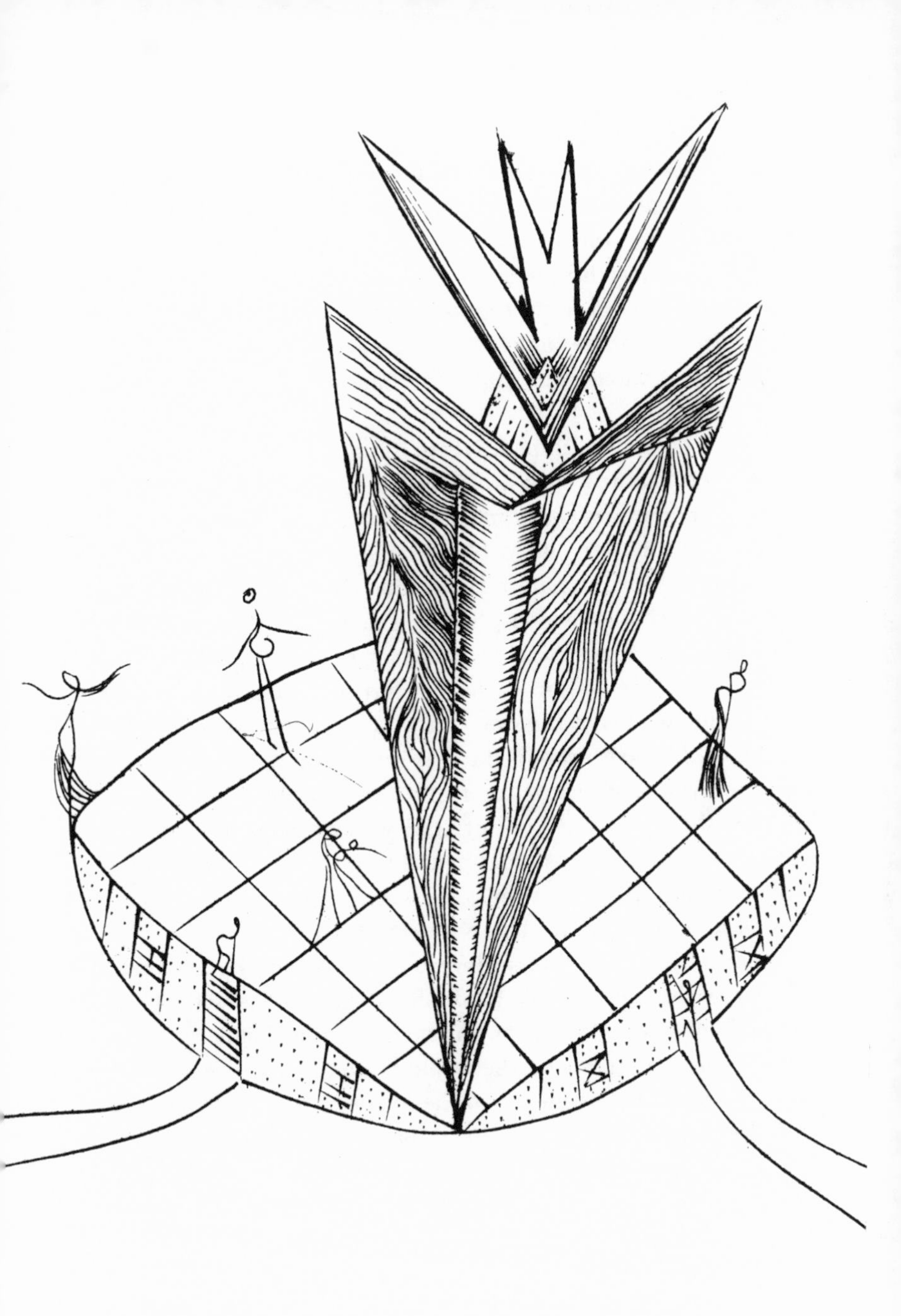

soon the three would find themselves on the one square until he chose to move away and leave them together.

What his game was no one knew, for he was content with the displacements and did not share in the developments. He would then stand in the corner of the room again and survey the movements with a semitone smile.

No one ever thought of displacing him, of introducing him to strangers.

But he thought it imperative to bring about an encounter between the bearded Irish architect and Djuna, because he had conceived a house for many moods, a house whose sliding panels made it one day very large for grandiose states of being, one day very small for intimate relationships. He had topped it with a removable ceiling which allowed the sky to play roof, and designed both a small spiral staircase for secret escapades and a vast one for exhibitionism. Besides, it turned on a pivot to follow the changing whims of the sun, and who but Djuna should know this house which corresponded to her many moods, to her smiling masks and refusal to show her night face, her shadows and her darkness, she who turned on artificial pivots always towards the light, who was adept at sliding panels to make womb enclosures suitable to intimate confessions, and equally capable of opening them all at once to admit the entire world.

Djuna smiled at the Chess Player's accuracy, and he left them standing on the square while the Irish architect began with silken mouthfuls of words to design this house around Djuna as if he were spewing a cocoon and she would leave the party like a snail with a house built around her to the image of her needs. On her black dress he was drawing a blue print.

On this square something was being constructed and so the Chess Player moved on, his eyes made of the glass one could look through without being seen and now he seized upon Faustin, the Zombie, the one who had died under the first blow struck at him by experience. Most of those who die like this in the middle of their life await a resuscitation, but Faustin awaited nothing: every line of his body sagged with acceptance, the growing weight of his flesh cushioned inertia, submission. The blood no longer circulated and one could see the crystal formations of fear and stagnation as in those species of fish living in the deepest waters without eyes, ears, fins, motion, shaped like loaves of bread, nourishing themselves through static cells of the skin. His one obsession was not to free himself of his death but to stand like a black sentinel at the gate and prevent others escaping from their traps. He lived among the artists, the rebels, never acquiescing in their rebellions, but waiting for the moment of Jay's fullest sunburst of enthusiasm to puncture it with irony, waiting for Lillian's wildest explosions to shame her as an exhibitionist, watching for Djuna's blurred absences from reality to point out her delinquencies from the present. His very expression set the stage for the murder; he had a way of bearing himself which was like the summation of all the prohibitions: do not trespass, do not smoke, do not spit, do not lean out of the window, no thoroughfare, do not speed.

With his black eyes and pale face set for homicide he waited in a corner. Wherever he was, a black moth would enter the room and begin its flights of mourning, black-gloved, black-creped, black-soled, inseminating the white walls with future sadnesses. The silence which followed his words clearly marked the withering effect of them and the time it took for the soil to bloom again.

Always at midnight he left, following a rigid compulsion, and the Chess Player knew he must act hastily if he were going to exploit the Zombie's death rays and test their effect upon the living.

He walked the Zombie towards the fullest bloom of all, towards the camellia face of Sabina which opened at a party like the crowned prize-winner of the flower shows and gave every man the sensation he held the tip of a breast in his teeth. Would Sabina's face close when the shadow of Faustin fell across it, when the black moth words and the monotonous voice fell upon her ears curtained intricately by her anarchic hair?

She merely turned her face away: she was too richly nourished with pollen, seeds and sap to wither before any man, even a dead one. Too much love and desire had flown through the curves of her body, too many sighs, whispers, lay folded in the cells of her skin. Through the many rivers of her veins too much pleasure had coursed; she was immune.

Faustin the Zombie felt bitterly defeated, for he loved to walk in the traces of Jay's large patterns and collect his discarded mistresses. He loved to live Jay's discarded lives, like a man accepting a second-hand coat. There was always a little warmth left in them.

From the moment of his defeat, he ceased to attend the Party, even in his role of zombie, and the Chess Player whose role it was to see that the Party was attended at all cost, even at the cost of pretending, was disturbed to see this shadowy figure walking now always between the squares, carefully setting his foot on that rim of Saturn, that rim of nowhere which surrounds all definite places. One fallen piece.

The Chess Player's eyes fell on Djuna but she had escaped all seizure by dissolving into the music. This was a game he could not play: giving yourself. Djuna gave herself in the most unexpected ways. She lived in the cities of the interior, she had no permanent abode. She was always arriving and leaving undetected, as through a series of trap doors. The life she led there no one knew anything about. It never reached the ears of reporters. The statisticians of facts could never interview her. Then unexpectedly, in a public place, in a concert hall, a dance hall, at a lecture, at a party, she gave the immodest spectacle of her abandon to Stravinsky, her body's tense identification with the dancer, or revealed a passionate interest in the study of phosphenes.

And now she sat very neatly shaped in the very outline of the guitar played by Rango, her body tuned by the keys of her fingers as if Rango were playing on the strands of her hair, of her nerves, and the black notes were issuing from the black pupils of her eyes.

At least she could be considered as attending the party: her eyes were not closed, as they had been a half hour earlier when she was telling the Chess Player about phosphenes: phosphenes are the luminous impressions and circles seen with the eyelids closed, after the sudden compression of the eyeball. "Try it!"

The guitar distilled its music. Rango played it with the warm sienna color of his skin, with the charcoal pupil of his eyes, with the underbrush thickness of his black eyebrows, pouring into the honey-colored box the flavors of the open road on which he lived his gypsy life: thyme, rosemary, oregano, marjoram and sage. Pouring into the resonant sound-box the sensual swing of his hammock hung across the gypsy-cart and the dreams born on his mattress of black horsehair.

Idol of the night clubs, where men and women barred the doors and windows, lit candles, drank alcohol, and drank from his voice and his guitar the potions and herbs of the open road, the charivaris of freedom, the drugs of leisure and laziness, the maypole dance of the fireflies, the horse's neighing fanfaronade, the fandangoes and ridottos of sudden lusts.

Shrunken breasts, vacillating eyes, hibernating virilities, all drank out of Rango's guitar and sienna voice. At dawn, not content with the life transfusion through cat guts, filled with the sap of his voice which had passed into their veins, at dawn the women laid hands upon his body like a tree. But at dawn Rango swung his guitar over his shoulder and walked away.

Will you be here tomorrow, Rango?

Tomorrow he might be playing and singing to his black horse's philosophically swaying tail on the road to the south of France.

Now arrived a very drunken Jay with his shoal of friends: five pairs of eyes wide open and vacant, five men wagging their heads with felicity because they are five. One a Chinese poet, tributary of Lao Tze; one Viennese poet, echo of Rilke; Hans the painter derived from Paul Klee, an Irish writer feebly stemming from Joyce. What they will become in the future does not concern them: at the present moment they are five praising each other and they feel strong and they are tottering with felicity.

They had had dinner at the Chinese restaurant, a rice without salt and meat with tough veins, but because of the shoal beatitude Jay proclaimed he had never eaten such rice, and five minutes later forgetting himself he said: "Rice is for the dogs!" The Chinese poet was hurt, his eyelids dropped humbly.

Now as they walked up the stairs he explained in neat phrases the faithfulness of the Chinese wife and Jay foamed with amazement: oh, such beautiful faithfulness! — he would marry a Chinese woman. Then the Chinese poet added: In China all tables are square. Jay almost wept with delight at this, it was the sign of a great civilization. He leaned over perilously and said with intimate secretiveness: In New Jersey when I was a boy tables were always round; I always hated round tables.

Their feet were not constructed for ascensions at the present moment; they might as well remain midway and call at Soutine's studio.

On the round stairway they collided with Stella susurrating in a tafetta skirt and eating fried potatoes out of a paper bag. Her long hair swayed as if she sat on a child's swing.

Her engaging gestures had lassoed an artist known for his compulsion to exhibit himself unreservedly, but he was not yet drunk enough and was for the moment content with strumming on his belt. Stella, not knowing what spectacle was reserved for her in his imagination, took the offering pose of women in Florentine paintings, extending the right hip like a holy water stand, both hands open as if inviting pigeons to eat from her palms, stylized, liturgical, arousing in Manuel the same impulse which had once made him set fire to a ballet skirt with a cigarette.

But Manuel was displaced by a figure who moved with stately politeness, his long hair patined with brilliantine, his face set in large and noble features by the men who carved the marble faces in the hall of fame.

He bowed graciously over women's hands with the ritualistic deliberateness of a Pope. His decrees, issued with handkissing, with soothing opening and closing of doors, extending of chairs, were nevertheless fatal: he held full power of decision over the delicate verdict: is it tomorrow's art?

No one could advance without his visa. He gave the passports to the future. Advance . . . or else: My dear man, you are a mere echo of the past.

Stella felt his handkissing charged with irony, felt herself installed in a museum *not* of modern art — blushed. To look at her in this ironic manner while scrupulously adhering to medieval salutations this man must know that she was one to keep faded flowers.

For he passed on with royal detachment and gazed seriously for relief at the steel and wood mobiles turning gently in the breeze of the future, like small structures of nerves vibrating in the air without their covering of flesh, the new cages of our future sorrows, so abstract they could not even contain a sob.

Jay was swimming against the compact stream of visitors looking for re-enforcement to pull out the Chinese poet who had stumbled into a very large garbage can in the front yard, and who was neatly folded in two, severely injured in his dignity. But he was arrested on his errand by the sight of Sabina and he thought why are there women in whom the sediment of experience settles and creates such a high flavor that when he had taken her he had also possessed all the unexplored regions of the world he had wanted to know, the men and women he would never have dared to encounter. Women whose bodies were a labyrinth so that when he was lying beside her he had felt he was taking a journey through the ancient gorge where Paracelsus dipped his sick people in fishing nets into lukewarm water, like a journey back into the womb, and he had seen several hundred feet above his head the little opening in the cathedral archway of the rocks through which the sun gleamed like a knife of gold.

But too late now to dwell on the panoramic, great voyage flavors of Sabina's body: the Chinese poet must be saved.

At this moment Sabina intercepted a look of tenderness between Jay and Lillian, a tenderness he had never shown her. The glance with which Lillian answered him was thrown around him very much like a safety net for a trapezist, and Sabina saw how Jay, in his wildest leaps, never leaped out of range of the net of protectiveness extended by Lillian.

The Chess Player noted with a frown that Sabina picked up her cape and made her way to the imitation Italian balcony. She was making a gradual escape; from balcony to balcony, she would break the friendly efforts made to detain her, and reach the exit. He could not allow this to go on, at a Party everyone should pursue nothing but his individual drama. Because Lillian and Jay had stood for a moment on the same square and Sabina had caught Jay leaping spuriously into the safety net of Lillian's protectiveness, now Sabina acted like one pierced by a knife and left the game for a balcony.

Where she stood now the noises of the Party could not reach her. She heard the wind and rain rushing through the trees like the lamentation of reeds in shallow tropical waters.

Sabina was lost.

The broken compass which inhabited her and whose wild fluctuations she had always obeyed, making for tumult and motion in place of direction, was suddenly fractured so that she no longer knew the relief of tides, ebbs and flows and dispersions.

She felt lost.

The dispersion had become too vast, too extended. For the first time a shaft of pain appeared cutting through the nebulous pattern.

Pain lies only in reflection, in awareness. Sabina had moved so fast that all pain had passed swiftly as through a sieve, leaving a sorrow like children's sorrows, soon forgotten, soon replaced by a new interest. She had never known a pause.

And suddenly in this balcony, she felt alone.

Her cape, which was more than a cape, which was a sail, which was the feelings she threw to the four winds to be swelled and swept by the wind in motion, lay becalmed.

Her dress was becalmed.

It was as if now she wore nothing that the wind could catch, swell and propel.

For Sabina, to be becalmed meant to die.

Jealousy had entered her body and refused to run through it like sand through an hourglass. The silvery holes of her sieve against sorrow granted her at birth through which everything passed through and out painlessly, had clogged. Now the pain had lodged itself inside of her.

She had lost herself somewhere along the frontier between her inventions, her stories, her fantasies, and her true self. The boundaries had become effaced, the tracks lost, she had walked into pure chaos, and not a chaos which carried her like the wild gallopings of romantic riders in operas and legends, but a cavalcade which suddenly revealed the stage prop: a papier-mâché horse.

She had lost her boat, her sails, her cape, her horse, her seven-league boots, and all of them at once, leaving her stranded on a balcony, among dwarfed trees, diminished clouds, a miserly rainfall.

In the semi-darkness of that winter evening, her eyes were

blurred. And then as if all the energy and warmth had been drawn inward for the first time, killing the senses, the ears, the touch, the palate, all movements of the body, all its external ways of communicating with the exterior, she suddenly felt a little deaf, a little blind, a little paralyzed; as if life, in coiling upon itself into a smaller, slower inward rhythm, were thinning her blood.

She shivered, with the same tremor as the leaves, feeling for the first time some small withered leaves of her being detaching themselves.

The Chess Player placed two people on a square.

As they danced a magnet pulled her hair and his together, and when they pulled their heads away, the magnet pulled their mouths together and when they separated the mouths, the magnet clasped their hands together and when they unclasped the hands their hips were soldered. There was no escape. When they stood completely apart then her voice spiralled around his, and his eyes were caught in the net grillage which barred her breasts.

They danced off the square and walked into a balcony.

Mouth meeting mouth, and pleasure striking like a gong, once, twice, thrice, like the beating wings of large birds. The bodies traversed by a rainbow of pleasure.

By the mouth they flowed into each other, and the little grey street ceased to be an impasse in Montparnasse. The balcony was now suspended over the Mediterranean, the Aegean sea, the Italian lakes, and through the mouth they flowed and coursed through the world.

While on the wall of the studio there continued to hang a large painting of a desert in smoke colors, a desert which parched the throat. Imbedded in the sand many little bleached bones of lovelessness.

"The encounter of two is pure, in two there is some hope of truth," said the Chess Player catching the long floating hair of Stella as she passed and confronting her with a potential lover.

Behind Stella hangs a painting of a woman with a white halo around her head. Anxiety had carved diamond holes through her body and her airiness came from this punctured faith through which serenity had flown out.

What Stella gave now was only little pieces of herself, pieces carefully painted in the form of black circles of wit, squares of yellow politeness, triangles of blue friendliness, or the mock orange of love: desire. Only little pieces from her external armor. What she gave now was a self which a man could only carry across the threshold of an abstract house with only one window on the street and this street a desert with little white bones bleaching in the sun.

Deserts of mistrust.

The houses are no longer hearths, they hang like mobiles turning to the changing breeze while they love each other like ice skaters on the top layers of their invented selves, blinded with the dust of attic memories, within the windowless houses of their fears.

The guests hang their coats upon a fragile structure like the bar upon which ballet dancers test their limb's wit.

The Party spreads like an uneasy octopus that can no longer draw in his tentacles to seize and strangle the core of its destructiveness.

In each studio there is a human being dressed in the full regalia of his myth fearing to expose a vulnerable opening, spreading not his charms but his defences, plotting to disrobe, somewhere along the night – his body without the aperture of the heart or his heart with a door closed to his body. Thus keeping one compartment for refuge, one uninvaded cell.

And if you feel a little compressed, a little cramped in your daily world, you can take a walk through a Chirico painting. The houses have only facades, so escape is assured; the colonnades, the volutes, valances extend into the future and you can walk into space.

The painters peopled the world with a new variety of fruit and tree to surprise you with the bitterness of what was known for its sweetness and the sweetness of what was known for its bitterness, for they all deny the world as it is and take you back to the settings and scenes of your dreams. You slip out of a Party into the past or the future.

This meandering led the Chess Player to stray from his geometrical duties, and he was not able to prevent a suicide. It was Lillian who stood alone on a square; Lillian who had begun the evening like an African dancer donning not only all of her Mexican silver jewelry but a dress of emerald green of a starched material which had a bristling quality like her mood.

She had moved from one to another with gestures of her hands inciting others to foam, to dance. She teased them out of their nonchalance or detachment. People would awaken from their lethargies as in a thunderstorm; stand, move, ignited, catching her motions, her hands beating a meringue of voices, a soufflé of excitement. When they were ready to follow her into some kind of tribal dance, she left them, to fall again into limpness or to walk behind her enslaved, seeking another electrical charge.

She could not even wait for the end of the Party to commit her daily act of destruction. So she stood alone in her square defended by her own bristles and began: "No one is paying any attention to me. I should not have worn this green dress: it's too loud. I've just said the wrong thing to Brancusi. All these people have accomplished something and I have not. They put me in a panic. They are all so strong and so sure of themselves. I feel exactly as I did in my dream last night: I had been asked to play at a concert. There were so many people. When I went to play, the piano had no notes, it was a lake, and I tried to play on the water and no sound came. I felt defeated and humiliated. I hate the way my hair gets wild. Look at Stella's hair so smooth and clinging to her face. Why did I tease her? She looked so tremulous, so frightened, as if pleading not to be hurt. Why do I rush and speak before thinking? My dress is too short."

In this invisible hara-kiri she tore off her dress, her jewels, tore off every word she had uttered, every smile, every act of the evening. She was ashamed of her talk, of her silences, of what she had given, and of what she had not given, to have confided and not to have confided.

And now it was done. A complete house-wrecking service. Every word, smile, act, silver jewel, lying on the floor, with the emerald green dress, and even Djuna's image of Lillian to which she had often turned for comfort, that too lay shattered on the ground. Nothing to salvage. A mere pile of flaws. A little pile of ashes from a bonfire of self-criticism.

The Chess Player saw a woman crumpling down on a couch as if her inner frame had collapsed, smiled at her drunkenness and took no note of the internal suicide.

Came the grey-haired man who makes bottles, Lawrence Vail, saying: "I still occasionally and quite frequently and very perpetually empty a bottle. This is apt to give one a guilty feeling. Is it not possible I moaned and mooned that I have neglected the exterior (of the bottle) for the interior (of the bottle)? Why cast away empty bottles? The spirits in the bottle are not necessarily the spirit of the bottle. The spirit of the spirits of the bottle are potent, potential substances that should not be discarded, eliminated in spleen, plumbing and hangover. Why not exteriorize these spirits on the body of the bottle. . . ."

The Chess Player saw it was going to happen.

He saw Djuna slipping off one of the squares and said: "Come here! Hold hands with Jay's warm winey white-trash friends. It is too early in the evening for you to be slipping off."

Djuna gave him a glance of despair, as one does before falling.

She knew it was now going to happen.

This dreaded mood which came, warning her by dimming the lights, muffling the sounds, effacing the faces as in great snowstorms.

She would be inside of the Party as inside a colored ball, being swung by red ribbons, swayed by indigo music. All the objects of the Fair around her – the red wheels, the swift chariots, the dancing animals, the puppet shows, the swinging trapezes, words and faces swinging, red suns bursting, birds singing, ribbons of laughter floating and catching her, teasing hands rustling in her hair, the movements of the dance like all the motions of love: taking, bending, yielding, welding and unwelding, all the pleasures of collisions every human being opening the cells of his gayety.

And then wires would be cut, lights grow dim, sounds muffled, colors paled.

At this moment, like the last message received through her inner wireless from the earth, she always remembered this scene: she was sixteen years old. She stood in a dark room brushing her hair. It was a summer night. She was wearing her nightgown. She leaned out of the window to watch a party taking place across the way.

The men and women were dressed in rutilant festive colors she had never seen before or was she dressing them with the intense light of her own dreaming for she saw their gayety, their relation to each other as something unparallelled in splendor. That night she yearned so deeply for this unattainable party, fearing she would never attend it, or else that if she did she would not be dressed in those heightened colors, she would not be so shining, so free. She saw herself attending but invisible, made invisible by timidity.

Now when she had reached this Party, where she had been visible and desired, a new danger threatened her: a mood which came and carried her off like an abductor, back into darkness.

This mood was always provoked by a phrase out of a dream: "This is not the place."

(What place? Was it the first party she wanted and none other, the one painted out of the darkness of her solitude?)

The second phrase would follow: "He is not the one."

Fatal phrase, like a black magic potion which annihilated the present. Instantly she was outside, locked out, thrust out by no one but herself, by a mood which cut her off from fraternity.

Merely by wishing to be elsewhere, where it might be more marvellous, made the near, the palpable seem then like an obstruction, a delay to the more marvellous place awaiting her, the more wonderful personage kept waiting. The present was murdered by this insistent, whispering, interfering dream, this invisible map constantly pointing to unexplored countries, a compass pointing to mirage.

But as quickly as she was deprived of ears, eyes, touch and placed adrift in space, as quickly as warm contact broke, she was granted another kind of ear, eye, touch, and contact.

She no longer saw the Chess Player as made of wood directed by a delicate geometric inner apparatus, as everyone saw him. She saw him before his crystallization, saw the incident which alchemized him into wood, into a chess player of geometric patterns. There, where a blighted love had made its first incision and the blood had turned to tree sap to become wood and move with geometric carefulness, there she placed her words calling to his warmth before it had congealed.

But the Chess Player was irritated. She addressed a man he did not recognize.

From the glass bastions of her city of the interior she could see all the excrescences, deformities, disguises, but as she moved among their hidden selves she incurred great angers.

"You demand we shed our greatest protections!"

"I demand nothing, I wanted to attend a Party. But the Party has dissolved in this strange acid of awareness which only dissolves the calluses, and I see the beginning."

"Stand on your square," said the Chess Player, "I shall bring you someone who will make you dance."

"Bring me one who will rescue me! Am I dreaming or dying? Bring me one who knows that between the dream and death there is only one frail step, one who senses that between this murder of the present by a dream, and death, there is only one shallow breath. Bring me one who knows that the dream without exit, without explosion, without awakening, is the passageway to the world of the dead! I want my dress torn and stained!"

A drunken man came up to her with a chair. Of all the chairs in the entire house he had selected a gold one with a red brocade top.

Why couldn't he bring me an ordinary chair?

To single her out for this hierarchic offering was to condemn her.

Now it was going to happen, inevitably.

The night and the Party had barely begun and she was being whisked away on a gold chair with a red brocade top by an abductor who would carry her back to the dark room of her adolescence, to the long white nightgown and hair brush, and to her dream of a Party that she could never attend.